# Dangerous Dukes

*Rakes about town*

Carole Mortimer introduces
London's most delectable dukes in her
latest Mills & Boon Historical mini-series.
But don't be fooled by their charm,
because beneath their lazy smiles they're
deliciously sexy—and highly dangerous!

Read about all the daring exploits
of these dangerous dukes in:

*Marcus Wilding: Duke of Pleasure*
Available as a
Mills & Boon Historical *Undone!* eBook

*Zachary Black: Duke of Debauchery*

*Darian Hunter: Duke of Desire*

*Rufus Drake: Duke of Wickedness*
Available as a
Mills & Boon Historical *Undone!* eBook

*Griffin Stone: Duke of Decadence*

And now…

*Christian Seaton: Duke of Danger*

## Author Note

It's so sad to think that I've written the final book in the ***Dangerous Dukes*** mini-series. I hope you've all enjoyed reading them as much as I've enjoyed writing them.

*Christian Seaton: Duke of Danger* is obviously Christian's unique love story, as he meets and falls in love with an outspoken Frenchwoman, Lisette Duprée, but there will be lots of secrets and intrigue along the way!

I also couldn't write this final book in the series without bringing back all the other Dangerous Dukes and telling you of their lives now with their own wonderful heroines.

Enjoy!

# CHRISTIAN SEATON: DUKE OF DANGER

Carole Mortimer

MILLS & BOON

First published in Great Britain 2015
By Mills & Boon, an imprint of HarperCollins*Publishers*
1 London Bridge Street, London, SE1 9GF

Large Print edition 2016

© 2015 Carole Mortimer

ISBN: 978-0-263-26277-3

Printed and bound in Great Britain
by CPI Antony Rowe, Chippenham, Wiltshire

**Carole Mortimer** was born and lives in the UK. She is married to Peter and they have six sons. She has been writing for Mills & Boon since 1978, and is the author of almost 200 books. She writes for both the Mills & Boon Historical and Modern lines. Carole is a *USA TODAY* bestselling author, and in 2012 was recognised by Queen Elizabeth II for her 'outstanding contribution to literature'.

Visit Carole at carolemortimer.co.uk or on Facebook.

### Books by Carole Mortimer

### Mills & Boon Historical Romance and Mills & Boon Historical *Undone!* eBooks

#### *Dangerous Dukes*

*Marcus Wilding: Duke of Pleasure* (Undone!)
*Zachary Black: Duke of Debauchery*
*Darian Hunter: Duke of Desire*
*Rufus Drake: Duke of Wickedness* (Undone!)
*Griffin Stone: Duke of Decadence*
*Christian Seaton: Duke of Danger*

#### *A Season of Secrets*

*Not Just a Governess*
*Not Just a Wallflower*
*Not Just a Seduction* (Undone!)

#### *Daring Duchesses*

*Some Like It Wicked*
*Some Like to Shock*
*Some Like It Scandalous* (Undone!)

#### *The Copeland Sisters*

*The Lady Gambles*
*The Lady Forfeits*
*The Lady Confesses*
*A Wickedly Pleasurable Wager* (Undone!)

#### M&B Regency *Castonbury Park* mini-series

*The Wicked Lord Montague*

Visit the Author Profile page
at millsandboon.co.uk for more titles.

To Peter, as always.

# Chapter One

*August 1815, Paris, France*

'Touch one hair upon her head, *monsieur*, and you are destined to meet your maker sooner than you might wish!'

It took every ounce of his indomitable will for Christian Seaton, Fifteenth Duke of Sutherland, not to react or turn to face the person who had just spoken softly behind him.

Not because he was disturbed by the threat itself; his reputation as one of the finest shots in England was not exaggerated, and few gentlemen could best him with the sword either.

Nor was he concerned by the barrel of the small pistol he currently felt pressed against the top of his spine through his clothing.

Or that the person making the threat was a woman who, judging by her voice, was a woman of mature years.

It was the fact that the threat had been spoken in accented English which caused him such inner unease...

As an agent for the English Crown, Christian had arrived secretly in Paris from England by boat just two nights ago and, as had been planned, he had immediately taken up residence as the Comte de Saint-Cloud—an old and extinct title of his mother's French family—in one of the grander houses situated alongside the Seine.

Since his arrival Christian had been careful not to speak any other language but French, which he could claim to speak like a native, once again courtesy of his maternal *grandmère*.

He had been especially careful to maintain that facade in the Fleur de Lis, a noisy and crowded tavern situated in one of the less salubrious areas of Paris.

That he was now being addressed in English brought into question whether this pretence in his identity had somehow been compromised.

He continued to maintain his comfortable slouch at a corner table of the noisy tavern as he answered the woman in French. 'Would you care to repeat your comment, *madame*?' he replied fluently in that language. 'I understand English a little, but I am afraid I do not speak it at all.'

'No?'

*'Non.'* Christian calmly answered the scornful taunt, although that feeling of unease continued to prickle inside him. 'I am the Comte de Saint-Cloud—at your service, *madame.*'

There was the briefest of pauses, as if the woman were considering challenging him on that claim. 'My mistake, Comte,' she finally murmured, before repeating her earlier warning in French.

'Ah.' He nodded. 'In that case, I confess I have no idea which "she" you are referring to.'

A loud *hmph* sounded behind him. 'Do not play games with me, Comte,' the woman growled. 'You have had eyes for no one but Lisette since the moment you arrived.'

Lisette...

So that was the name of the beautiful young

woman serving the tables situated on the other side of this crowded and noisy room.

Oh, yes, Christian knew exactly which 'she' this woman was referring to. Which of the serving wenches he had been unable to take his eyes off of for more than a minute or two since he had entered the tavern an hour ago.

And he was not alone in that interest, having noticed that several other well-dressed gentlemen in the room were also watching the young woman, if less openly than he.

The reason for those gentlemen's slyness now become apparent to Christian—obviously they knew better than to openly show their admiration for the red-haired beauty, for fear of having a pistol pressed against their own spine.

He gave another glance across the tavern to where the young woman had been kept busy all evening serving drinks to the raucous patrons. She was unlike any other tavern wench Christian had ever seen—tiny and slender, with pretty red curls, hidden for the main part beneath a black lace cap, she was also dressed more conservatively than the other serving wenches, in a long-sleeved and high-necked black gown.

A mourning gown…?

Whatever her reason for wearing black, it did not detract in the slightest from the girl's ethereal beauty. Rather it seemed to emphasise it; her hands and neck were slender, her heart-shaped face as pale and smooth as alabaster and dominated by huge long-lashed blue eyes.

She had also, Christian had observed with satisfaction, managed to neatly and cheerfully avoid any of the slyly groping male hands that had tried to take advantage of her as she placed jugs of ale down on the tables.

Unfortunately, Christian had not seen her until after he was already seated, his own table being served by a buxom and flirtatious brunette, and so preventing him from as yet finding opportunity to speak to the lovely Lisette.

A situation which Christian had intended changing before the night was over; a dalliance with one of the Fleur de Lis' serving wenches would be the perfect means by which he might visit this tavern often, without the regularity of those visits being remarked upon.

He gave a lazy shrug now, again without turning to look at the woman behind him. 'All of the ladies working here are very pretty, *madame*.' Once again he continued the conversation in French.

'But you have eyes for only one,' the woman rasped in the same language.

'Surely a gentleman is allowed to look, *madame*?'

'One such as you does not just look for long,' she said scornfully.

Christian was every inch the gentleman, known amongst English society for his charm and evenness of temper; indeed, he had long and deliberately nurtured that belief. But that was not to say that he did not have a temper, because he most certainly did; he simply chose to reveal it only to those who were deserving of it and on the occasions when it was most warranted.

But whether the French Comte de Saint-Cloud or the English Duke of Sutherland, he was obviously a gentleman, and this woman's insults and overfamiliarity were deserving of such a set-down. 'I take exception to your remark, *madame*.' Christian's tone was icy-cold, something that those who knew him well would have known to beware of.

Whatever the woman standing behind him knew of him, she obviously did not know the nature of him at all.

At least it was to be hoped that she did not...

'One has only to look at the way you are dressed, at *you*, to know you are nothing but a rake and a libertine. *Coureur!*' she added disgustedly.

While it might be safer for this woman to believe Christian was a rake, and the 'womaniser' she had just spat at him, than for her to have any doubts as to his identity as the Comte de Saint-Cloud, he still took exception to the insult. 'On what grounds do you base such an accusation, *madame*?' His tone had grown even chillier.

'On the grounds that you have been undressing my...niece with your eyes for this past hour, *monsieur*!' she came back disgustedly.

Her *niece*?

The beautiful girl, Lisette, was the *niece* of the woman standing behind him with a pistol pressed against his spine? Surely that claim did not make sense unless—

Unless…?

Very aware of that pistol at his back, Christian carefully sat forward, his movements measured as he turned just as slowly to face his accuser. His brows rose slightly as he instantly recognised her as being none other than Helene Rousseau, the owner of this Parisian tavern.

The very same woman who was both the reason for his clandestine visit to Paris and for his presence in the Fleur de Lis tavern this evening.

Helene Rousseau was the older sister of André Rousseau, the man known to have been a French spy during the year he had spent in England as tutor to a young English gentleman.

A year during which André Rousseau had also gathered together a ring of treasonous co-conspirators amongst the servants of the English aristocracy, as well as some high-ranking members of that society itself. Their aim had been to assassinate England's Prince Regent, as well as the other heads of the Alliance, and so throw those countries into a state of chaos and confusion, allowing Napoleon, newly escaped from his incarceration on Elba, to march triumphantly back into Paris unopposed.

Christian had been one of the agents for the Crown who had managed to foil that assassination plot on Prinny. But not before André Rousseau lay dead in the street outside this very tavern, killed by the hand of one of Christian's closest friends.

Christian was in Paris now because it was suspected that Rousseau's sister had taken over as head of that resistance movement following the death of her brother. That she and her cohorts were still determined to undermine the English government, whilst working with those co-conspirators in England, by fair means or foul—and their methods had been very foul indeed—to find a way of releasing the Corsican upstart for a second time.

Indeed Christian, and several of his friends, had only days ago prevented news of the date and destination of Napoleon's second incarceration from being revealed, when it was believed that a second attempt would have been made to effect the Corsican's escape.

Nowhere in Christian's information on Helene Rousseau had there ever been mention of her having a niece.

The same young and beautiful woman whom Christian had been admiring for this past hour or more…

A young and beautiful woman who wore black because she was in mourning for her dead father, the French spy André Rousseau? As far as Christian was aware, Helene Rousseau had no other siblings.

His eyes narrowed on the Frenchwoman. Also dressed in black out of respect for her dead brother? 'I apologise if I have caused you any offence, *madame*.' He gave a courtly bow as he stood up. 'I assure you I meant none.'

Helene Rousseau was a woman of about forty, tall and voluptuous where her niece was tiny and slender, and the older woman had only a touch of red in her blonde hair; surely Christian could be forgiven for not having previously made the connection between an aunt and niece who were so different in appearance?

Especially as there had never been any information of André Rousseau having a daughter.

Hard blue eyes looked up at him scornfully as the female owner of the tavern continued to hold the small pistol at a level with his broad chest. 'A man such as you would not be in such a lowly tavern as this one, *monsieur*, if you were not looking to corrupt one of my girls.'

Christian raised a blond brow. 'Surely it is for those "girls" to decide for themselves as to whether or not they would see my attentions as corruption…or pleasure?'

'Not if your choice is to be Lisette.' Helene Rousseau looked at him with all the challenging hauteur of a duchess.

Christian bit back his impatience with this woman's temerity, knowing it would not serve his purpose to antagonise her further; his intention this evening, to be taken for just another gentleman bent on pleasure, had instead incurred this woman's notice as well as her wrath. Both of them he would rather have avoided at this stage of his mission. 'I have given my apology if I have caused you any offence—'

'I believe Claude wishes your presence in the kitchen, Helene,' a huskily soft voice interrupted them.

A huskily soft voice that, Christian discovered when his gaze moved to Helene Rousseau's side, belonged to none other than the beautiful Lisette herself...

Lisette had noticed the handsome gentleman with the lavender-coloured eyes the moment he entered the tavern earlier this evening; indeed, he was the sort of gentleman of whom any woman would take note.

He was exceedingly tall, with tousled overlong blond hair. The perfect fit of his black superfine coat over broad and muscled shoulders must surely be the work of the best tailors in Paris. As were the pantaloons tailored to his long and muscled legs. His black Hessians were so highly polished Lisette was sure she would be able to see her face in them if she cared to look.

But it was the hard masculine beauty of the

man's face which drew the eye; a smooth, high brow, sharply etched cheekbones, his nose long and aristocratic, and a sensual and decadent mouth that was not too thin and yet not too full either, above a surprisingly hard and uncompromising jaw.

The man's most arresting feature by far was his eyes—Lisette did not believe she had ever seen eyes of such an unusual shade of lavender before—fringed by thick and curling lashes.

Eyes which she had sensed watching her this past hour, even as she went about the business of serving the many and increasingly inebriated customers…

The tavern was unusually crowded this evening, which was the only reason Helene had asked for Lisette's help; usually the older woman did not allow her anywhere near the men who patronised this bawdy tavern.

Lisette had not initially noticed Helene approaching or speaking with the lavender-eyed gentleman; it was only when she could no longer feel the intensity of his gaze upon her that she had glanced across the room and seen the two in conversation. Even across the width of the tavern Lisette had been able to sense the tension of that conversation, her eyes widening in alarm as the gentleman moved and she saw that Helene held a pistol in her hand, and that pistol was pointed at the gentleman's chest.

Quite what that gentleman had done to warrant such attention Lisette had no idea. As far as she was aware, he had not behaved in a rowdy or licentious manner, but remained quietly seated at his table without engaging with any of the tavern's other customers. Nor had he been overfamiliar with Brigitte on the occasions she had served him with one of the tavern's better wines.

'I am Christian Beaumont, the Comte de Saint-Cloud, at your service, *mademoiselle.*' That gentleman now gave her a polite bow.

Just as if Helene were not still pointing a gun at the broad elegance of his chest!

'Lisette Duprée.' She gave an abrupt curtsy, unable, now that she was standing so close to the gentleman, to look away from the intensity of that beautiful lavender gaze.

Christian repressed his smile of satisfaction

at Helene Rousseau herself having effectively made the formal introductions possible. A formality that would allow him to more easily approach and speak to the lovely Lisette in future.

His gaze narrowed as he turned to look at the older woman. 'Please do not let us delay you any further when you are so obviously needed in the kitchen, *madame*.'

Helene Rousseau's mouth tightened even as she deftly stowed the pistol away in the folds of her gown. 'You will remember all that I have said to you tonight, my lord.' It was a warning, not a question.

Christian had every intention of remembering each and every word this woman spoke to him. Of dissecting it. Analysing it. In readiness for the report he would eventually take back with him to England.

And if it should transpire that Helene Rousseau was indeed behind the recent kidnapping of an innocent child, and the abduction and ill treatment of an equally innocent young lady, in order to try to blackmail information from the English government in the former, and repress information in the latter, then he feared there could be only one outcome to Helene Rousseau's future.

An outcome that would result in the lovely Lisette being in mourning for both her aunt and her father.

'I assure you, *madame*, my memory is impeccable,' Christian answered Helene Rousseau softly.

The older woman gave him a long and warning stare before turning to Lisette, the hardness of her features softening slightly as she looked at the younger woman. 'You must not linger here, Lisette, when there are customers needing to be served.'

'As you say, Helene.' Lisette's dark auburn lashes were lowered demurely as her aunt gave Christian one last warning glance before departing with a swish of her skirts. In the direction of the kitchen, it was to be hoped.

Christian found it curious that the younger woman addressed the older one by her first name rather than as her *tante*. Adding to the mystery of this relationship, that no amount of watching and spying on both André Rousseau before the man's death, and Helene Rousseau in the months since, had managed to discover, let alone explain.

'Would you care to sit down and join me, *mademoiselle*?' Christian held back one of the chairs at his table.

Lisette eyed him curiously. 'I am at work, Comte, not leisure.' And she would not have frequented a tavern such as this one even if she were.

Until just a few months ago, Lisette had lived all of her nineteen years in the French countryside, far away from any city, let alone Paris. It had been a shock for her to suddenly find herself living in such a place as this tavern, after the death of the couple she had believed to be her parents.

*Believed* to be her parents...

The truth of the matter had only emerged on the day of their funeral, when a carriage had arrived at their farm late that afternoon and a tall and haughty blonde woman had stepped down, a look of complete disdain on her face as she stepped carefully across the farmyard to the house.

Learning that this woman was actually her mother had been even more of a shock to Lisette than losing the couple she had believed to be her parents.

Helene Rousseau claimed Lisette had been fostered with the Duprées since she was a very young baby, and that they had been sent money every month for her upkeep.

Having never so much as set eyes on this woman before that day, Lisette had been disinclined to believe her at first. Although she could think of no reason why anyone would want to make such a false claim; Lisette was not rich, and even the Duprées' farm had been left to their nephew rather than Lisette.

The reason for which had become obvious with the arrival of Helene Rousseau.

The older woman had clearly been prepared for Lisette's disbelief and had brought letters with her that she had received every month from the Duprées, in relation to Lisette's health and well-being.

It was the non-appearance of this month's letter that had alerted Helene Rousseau to the fact that something was amiss on the Duprée farm; enquiries had informed her that both of the Duprées had died when a tree had fallen during a storm and landed on that part of the farmhouse where the Duprées' bedchamber was situated.

Lisette had only needed to read three of those letters sent by the Duprées to Helene Rousseau to know that the older woman was telling the truth; Lisette was indeed the other woman's illegitimate daughter.

What had followed still seemed like something of a dream to Lisette—or perhaps it might better be described as a nightmare?

Her belongings had all been quickly packed into a trunk—Helene Rousseau had disdained the idea of spending so much as a single night at the farm—after which Lisette had been bundled into the coach with the other woman before then travelling through the night to Paris.

If Helene Rousseau had found the sight and sounds of the farmyard unacceptable, then Lisette had been rendered numb by the noise and dirt of Paris as the carriage drove through the early morning streets.

Tradesmen were already about, hawking their wares amongst the people lying drunk in shop doors and alleyways, several overpainted and scantily dressed ladies slinking off into those same alleyways as the carriage passed by them.

The tavern Helene Rousseau owned and ran had been even more of a shock, situated as it was in one of the poorer areas of the city, with patrons to match.

It had been no hardship at all for Lisette to remain apart from such surroundings. To keep mainly in the bedchamber assigned to her by Helene—even all these weeks later Lisette could not think of the older woman as anything more than the woman who had given birth to her before then abandoning her for the next nineteen years. As far as Lisette was concerned, sending money for her daughter's upkeep did not equate to love on Helene Rousseau's part, only a sense of responsibility; the other woman had made no attempt in all of those years to actually see or speak with her daughter.

Given a choice, Lisette would not have travelled to Paris with Helene Rousseau at all. But she did not have a choice. How could she, when she had no money of her own, her foster parents were both dead and their nephew had made it clear that she could not continue to live on the farm once he had moved there with his wife and large family?

But within days of arriving in Paris, Lisette had come to hate it with a vengeance. It was smelly and dirty, and the people she occasionally met out in the streets or the tavern were not much better. And Helene Rousseau proved to be a cold and distant woman with whom Lisette had nothing in common but her birth.

There was also deep unrest still amongst the Parisian people, who had first had a king, then an emperor, then a king again, and then again an emperor, only for that emperor to then once again be deposed and their king returned to them.

Such things had not affected Lisette when she'd lived on the farm with the Duprées. There they had only been concerned with caring for

the animals, and the setting of and then bringing in of the harvest each year.

But political intrigues seemed to abound in
Paris, with neighbour speaking out against
neighbour, often with dire consequences.

Lisette also strongly suspected there were
meetings held in one of the private rooms above
the tavern, in which that political unrest was
avidly and passionately discussed. Meetings over
which Helene Rousseau presided…

'Then perhaps you might meet with me outside
and join me for a late supper at my home when
you have finished your work for the night…?'

Lisette's eyes widened in shock as she looked
up at the handsome gentleman who did not seem
as if he should be in such a place as this lowly
tavern at all, let alone asking one of the serving
women if she would meet him for supper.

No doubt he was one of those gentlemen the
Duprées had warned her of when she'd reached
her sixteenth birthday and had shown signs of
developing a womanly figure. Gentlemen who
gave not a care if they disgraced an innocent,
before continuing merrily on their way.

'I am afraid that will not be possible, Monsieur la Comte—' She broke off as the lavender-eyed Comte stepped forward to prevent her from leaving. 'I must return to my work, *monsieur*,' she insisted firmly.

Christian found that he had no wish for Lisette to return to her work. Indeed, he discovered he was not favourably inclined to this young and beautiful woman working in this tavern at all.

It was a lowly, bawdy place, where he had just observed a man thrusting his hand down the low-cut bodice of a barmaid's gown, before popping that breast out completely so that he might fondle and suckle a rosy nipple. Where in another shadowy corner of the tavern he could see another couple, the woman's skirts pushed up to her waist, the man's breeches unfastened, as the two of them actually fornicated in front of all who cared to watch.

Christian, for all his previous sins, most certainly did not care to view so unpleasant a sight.

Indeed, he had begun to find the whole atmosphere of this tavern to be overly lewd and oppressive.

And this delicate woman certainly did not belong in such a place, no matter what her biological connection to the patroness might be.

He curled his fingers lightly about the slenderness of Lisette's arm. 'I will be waiting outside in my carriage for you to join me from midnight onwards—'

'I cannot, *monsieur*.' Her eyes had filled with alarm. 'Tonight or any other night.'

'I mean you no harm, Lisette.' Christian sighed his frustration with her obvious distrust. 'You must know that you do not belong here?'

Tears now swam in those exquisite blue eyes. 'I have nowhere else to go, *monsieur*.'

Rescuing an obvious damsel in distress was not part of Christian's mission. Indeed, his superiors in government would say it was the opposite of his purpose here. Most especially when that damsel was the niece of the woman—and quite possibly the daughter of the rabble-rouser André Rousseau?—he had come here to observe.

He released her arm reluctantly. 'I will be waiting outside for you in my carriage from midnight anyway, just in case you should change your mind…'

'I cannot, *monsieur.*' She cast a furtive glance towards the kitchen as the door swung open and Helene Rousseau strode back into the noisy tavern, her shrewd eyes narrowing as she saw Christian and Lisette were still standing together in conversation. 'I must go.' Lisette stepped hastily away from him. 'For your own sake, *monsieur,* I advise you do not come here again,' she added in a whisper.

Christian considered that warning some minutes later as he sat in his carriage on the way back to his house beside the Seine, and he could come to only one conclusion.

That the lovely Lisette was frightened of her aunt…

# Chapter Two

Lisette went about the rest of her work in a daze following the Comte's departure just minutes after their conversation came to an abrupt end.

In response to her warning, she hoped.

Although he had not appeared to be the sort of gentleman who would frighten easily.

As she was frightened.

The Comte de Saint-Cloud was perfectly correct in his concern for her well-being here, with the drunkards and bawds. Much as Helene might try to protect her.

But what else did the Comte have to offer her, besides supper and no doubt a seduction within his home; he might be wealthier and more highly born than the usual patrons of the Fleur de Lis, but he was no more to be trusted than the other nen who came here, who would all willingly hrow up her skirts and take her innocence, given the opportunity and the chance to escape from Helene's sharp-eyed gaze.

The Comte might do it more gracefully, and no doubt in pleasanter surroundings, but he would still take what Lisette did not wish to give. Before walking away unconcernedly to rejoin others of his class and forgetting completely the young woman whom he had seduced. And ruined.

The fact that he had frequented such a tavern as this at all was suspect. And surely indication of his intention to find a woman he might take to bed for the night, before having one of his servants show her the door in the morning, when he had no further use for her?

Lisette knew that could be the only possible reason for such a fine and titled gentleman to so much as enter a lowly tavern such as this one.

And yet for just a few moments, a minute perhaps, something had burgeoned inside her chest—a temptation to accept his offer of joining him for a late supper—in the hope that he might offer to take her away from this lowly place, which she hated to her very soul.

'You might as well stop mooning over the Comte,' Helene sneered several hours later, after having thrown out the last of her drunken customers into the alleyway at the back of the tavern, before locking the door behind her. 'He will not be returning here.'

Lisette looked at the older woman searchingly, easily noting the satisfaction in Helene's expression. 'How can you be so sure…?'

Hard blue eyes flashed a warning. 'You will not question me as to my…methods, Lisette.'

Her alarm deepened. 'I am sure Monsieur le Comte meant no harm when he spoke to me earlier.'

'I believe it is past time you retired to your bedchamber, Lisette,' Helene dismissed. 'You have been most helpful this evening, but I do not think we will repeat the experience.'

'But—'

'Go to bed now, Lisette.' The older woman

snapped her impatience as a knock now sounded softly on the closed back door of the tavern.

Lisette bit back her next comment, that discreet knock on the door warning her that this was one of those nights when Helene was to have another of her meetings.

Clandestine meetings, with men—and women?—who either did not want to be seen frequenting the tavern or openly associating with Helene Rousseau. Or perhaps both? The Fleur de Lis and its customers were certainly not for the faint-hearted, or those members of society who should not even know such a woman as Helene Rousseau existed, let alone be calling upon her in the dark of night.

None of which helped to dispel Lisette's concerns for the welfare of the Comte de Saint-Cloud.

She had learned these past weeks that Helene was a powerful woman in these shadowed alleyways of Paris, with a knowledge of most, if not all, of the thieves and murderers that frequented them. It would be the simplest thing in the world for the older woman to request the assistance—

after silver had exchanged hands, of course—of any one of those cut-throats in her desire to ensure the Comte de Saint-Cloud did not return.

Could not return.

'Certainly, Helene.' She made a curtsy before taking a lit candle and hurrying up the stairs to her bedchamber, only to then pace the small room restlessly as she tried to decide what she should do next.

She really could not allow the Comte de Saint-Cloud to come to harm just because he had dared to speak with her.

She had heard the murmur of voices in the hallway outside some minutes ago, followed by a door closing, which meant that Helene would now be kept occupied with her late night callers. If Lisette was very quiet, she could move softly along the hallway and down the stairs, leave a window open downstairs at the back of the tavern ready for her to climb into upon her return, and then—

And then what?

The Comte had said his house was situated by the river, but just the thought of being out alone at night in Paris was enough to cause a quiver of fear to run the length of Lisette's spine. These streets were unsafe for a lone woman in the daytime; at night she would be an easy target for much more than the thieves and bawds.

And the Comte de Saint-Cloud?

Her thoughts always came back to him, and the look of determination on Helene's face when she had said he would not be returning to the tavern. Such certainty of purpose could surely mean only one thing? Nor did Lisette make the mistake of underestimating Helene's ability to carry through with that purpose; many of the men who frequented the tavern, hard and callous men, were obviously in awe of the Fleur de Lis' patroness.

Lisette could not bear to think of the handsome Comte's lavender-coloured eyes closing forever.

Just as she could not continue to stay here in her bedchamber, acting the coward, when even now Helene's cut-throats might be closing in for the kill.

Lisette's spine straightened with a resolve she could not allow to waver as she pulled on her black bonnet and gathered up her black cloak—mourning clothes for the uncle she had never met—before quietly opening the door to her bedchamber and peering out to ensure that the hallway was empty. Assured it was so, she quietly slipped from the room and down the stairs. With any luck she would be able to find and visit the Comte's home, issue a warning and return to the tavern before Helene was any the wiser.

If not…

Lisette did not care to think of what might happen if she was too late to warn Monsieur le Comte.

Or of Helene's fury if Lisette did not return to the tavern before her absence was discovered.


Christian stood in the shadows of a doorway, a safe enough distance from the Fleur de Lis, but close enough that he was able to see the dozen or so gentlemen and two ladies, who had entered through the back door of that establishment during the past half an hour.

He was under no illusions as to the reason for their clandestine visit, knew that he must have stumbled upon one of the secret meetings of Helene Rousseau and her co-conspirators.

Stumbled, because Helene Rousseau was not the reason Christian had come back to the tavern tonight.

He had returned briefly to his house by the Seine after leaving the tavern earlier, going inside to his bedchamber so that he might change into dark clothing, before going out again. He had ordered his groom to wait with the carriage several streets away from the Fleur de Lis, before wrapping his dark cloak about him to move stealthily through the pungent and filthy alleyways to the doorway across and down the street from the tavern.

The tavern was in darkness apart from a single candle burning in one of the bedchambers above, which, from the slightness of the silhouette of a person he could see pacing back and forth past the curtained window, might possibly be the bedchamber of the lovely Lisette.

When even that candle was extinguished just minutes later, the tavern was left in complete darkness.

And Christian with a feeling of disappointment.

It had been too much to hope for, of course, that Lisette would change her mind and join him for a late supper. She did not know him, nor did she seem the type of young lady who would sneak out of her aunt's home in the middle of the night with the intention of dining alone with a gentleman. Even without her eagle-eyed aunt acting as her protector.

That look of innocence, and the tears that had shone in those huge blue eyes earlier when Lisette had told him she had 'nowhere else to go', could all be an act, of course. Nothing more than the clever machinations of an innocent-looking whore in search of a rich protector. Christian was sure he would not be the first gentleman to fall for such an act.

Yet there had been a sincerity to Lisette Duprée. An indication, perhaps, that her innocence might be genuine.

And Christian could just be the biggest fool in Paris for giving that young woman so much as a second thought. Indeed, Helene Rousseau's warning earlier, in regard to his staying away from her niece, might all be part of the ruse to pique and hold his interest, rather than the opposite.

There was also that disturbing moment to consider when Helene Rousseau had initially spoken to him in English. A test, perhaps, to see if he would respond in kind? Or possibly because she already knew he was not the Comte de Saint-Cloud?

If that was the case, then Christian's presence in Paris was a complete waste of time, and he would learn nothing. Except perhaps to feel the sharp end of a blade piercing his back when he least expected it.

Even more reason for Christian to concentrate on the meeting now taking place within the tavern, and the identity of the people present.

Rather than, as he had been doing, imagining how Lisette would look as she lay in her bed…

Would she be dressed demurely in a night-rail, or did she sleep naked?

Would her breasts be tipped by rosy nipples or darker plum-coloured ones?

And would the silky thatch between her thighs be as vibrant a red as the curls—?

'Monsieur le Comte…?'

It would be an understatement, considering the direction of his thoughts, to say that Christian was startled to hear the sound of Lisette's soft and huskily enquiring voice beside him.

Startled and not a little annoyed with himself for being so distracted by thoughts of this beautiful young woman that he had not even noticed her leaving the tavern, let alone approaching him. Such inattentiveness could easily get a man killed.

Christian gathered his thoughts as he turned to face her, approving of the fact that she at least wore dark clothing, as he did, the hood of her cloak pulled up over her bonnet, hiding the brightness of her hair. 'I am gratified to see you have changed your mind about joining me for supper, *mademoiselle*,' he answered her flirtatiously.

'We cannot stay here, where we might be seen at any moment, *monsieur*,' she came back urgently.

'No, of course not,' Christian readily accepted as he took a firm hold of her arm. He might now have to abandon his interest in the identity of the people who had so recently entered the tavern so surreptitiously but he had the next best thing: Helene Rousseau's niece. 'My carriage is waiting for us—'

'Oh, no, *monsieur*, I cannot come with you. I wished only to—'

'Hush!' Christian warned sharply as he pulled her into his arms and pressed her back into the shadows of the doorway, having noticed that several cloaked figures were now leaving the tavern.

*'Monsieur!'* Lisette protested indignantly.

'Hush—'

*'Monsieur*, I must protest—'

Christian could think of only one way he might prevent Lisette from alerting others to their presence here with her verbal indignation at his manhandling of her.

He took it.

Lisette's protests died in her throat, to be replaced by surprise and then pleasure, as the Comte took masterful possession of her lips with his own.

She had never been kissed before, nor had she ever dreamed that her first kiss would be with such a man as the handsome Comte de Saint-Cloud.

That he was an expert in such things came as no surprise to her; he was at least a dozen years her senior, and there was about him an air of ease and sophistication that spoke of his knowledge of women.

Even knowing that, Lisette was immediately lost to everything but the wonder of Christian Beaumont's mouth on hers. His arms were firm about her as he held her against the hardness of his body, and the warmth of his tongue dared a caress across her lips to part them and deepen the kiss.

Heart pounding, Lisette's hands moved to cling to the folds of his evening cloak, as she felt herself completely overwhelmed by the emotions coursing through her body: excitement and pleasure. The latter manifested itself in the tightening of the bodice of her gown, as if her breasts were swelling, the rosy tips tingling, and there was an unfamiliar but not unpleasant warmth blossoming between her thighs.

It was singularly the most wonderful experience of her short lifetime, beyond any imagining, beyond—

The Comte brought the kiss to an abrupt end as he lifted his mouth from hers. 'Do not speak, Lisette,' he warned softly against her ear. 'Whatever happens, do not speak.'

*Whatever happens...?*

Lisette felt too dazed still to understand what he meant by that. What did he imagine was going to happen? A kiss was a kiss, but anything more than that was unthinkable. And if the Comte thought— If he imagined for one moment—

'Feel like sharing, *mon ami*?'

'For the price I paid for her? *Non.*' The Comte turned his head to answer the intruder with a dismissive laugh, at the same time as the bulk of his body managed to keep Lisette shielded from any gaze that might try to pry any further into the doorway. 'I intend to take my money's worth and more!'

*'Bon chance!'* another man called out laughingly as the two continued on their way.

Lisette's face paled as she listened to the exchange between the three men, shocked by the earthiness of the conversation but also realising the Comte must have been protecting her from the attentions of the other men when he pushed her into the doorway.

At the same time she felt disappointed to realise that the Comte had kissed her for the same reason. It was a little humiliating to realise how much she had enjoyed the kiss when, to the Comte, it had only been a means of silencing her.

She pushed determinedly against the muscled chest pinning her in the doorway. 'I believe we are alone again now, *monsieur*. You may release me,' she instructed sharply as she failed to shift him by so much as an inch.

Christian had no desire to 'release' Lisette. Indeed, the opposite. He wanted to kiss her again, this time without the distraction of the approach of the two gentlemen he had noted leaving the tavern; Helene Rousseau's meeting was obviously over for tonight. Which meant that more of the co-conspirators would shortly be leaving the tavern too.

'We need to leave here, Lisette.'

'I came only to warn you—'

'Warn me?' Christian questioned sharply as he stepped back slightly to look down at her. Not that he could see very much; the streets were dark, and the doorway even darker.

'My—Helene did not take kindly to your attentions to me earlier this evening, *monsieur*—'

'Christian. Call me Christian,' he instructed shortly, having duly noted Lisette's slight hesitation after 'my'.

'It is not permissible—'

'I just kissed you, Lisette,' he drawled. 'I believe that now makes many things between the two of us "permissible".'

She drew in a soft gasp. 'It is ungentlemanly of you to talk of such things.'

Christian wanted to do more than talk about them; the throb of his arousal told him he wanted to kiss Lisette again, and keep on kissing every inch of her as he made full and pleasurable love to her. Which, given their circumstances, was beyond reckless of him.

Not only were they in a precarious position out here where they might be seen together, but also he still did not know whether Lisette was all that she appeared to be, or if she was working in cahoots with her aunt. Until he did know he would be wise to treat her, and anything she said to him, with suspicion.

Which would be easier for him to do if only she did not have those deep blue eyes he wanted to drown in, and those soft and delectable lips he wished to kiss and keep on kissing…

'We cannot stay here, Lisette.' Christian took a firm hold of her arm to pull her along at his side as he stepped out of the doorway and began to walk quickly away from the tavern. 'My carriage is but a short distance away. We will talk again once we are inside and well away from prying eyes and ears.'

'Please—I must return to the tavern before I am missed,' Lisette protested as she almost had to run to keep up with the Comte's much longer strides or risk falling over onto the dirty cobbles beneath her feet.

The Comte either did not hear her or chose to ignore her as he continued to stride purposefully, and knowledgeably, down several alleyways Lisette had not even known were there, despite having lived in Paris for some weeks now.

A carriage waited in the shadows of one of the streets, and it was towards this vehicle that the Comte now guided her as a groom jumped quickly down to hold the door open for them both to get inside.

Lisette held back from entering the carriage. 'It is impossible for me to go with you, *monsieur—Umph!*' The rest of Lisette's protest was cut off as the Comte de Saint-Cloud unceremoniously picked her up in his arms and deposited her inside the carriage before tersely instructing the groom to move on as he joined her and the door was firmly closed behind him.

A lantern lit the inside of the heavily curtained carriage—which was perhaps the reason Lisette had not been able to see the light before now?—allowing her to appreciate the plushness of the interior.

And the man now seated opposite her...

His hair shone like burnished gold in the lamplight, those lavender eyes narrowed in a face that was far too handsome for any woman's comfort. Especially so, when he had kissed that woman a short time ago and she was now alone with him in his carriage.

'You take liberties, *monsieur*.' Lisette glared across at the Comte as she now straightened her bonnet from where it had been knocked askew when he had picked her up and thrust her inside the carriage.

Some of the Comte's tension seemed to ease and he relaxed back against the upholstery as the carriage began to move forward. 'You are the one who came looking for me, Lisette, remember.'

She did remember. And she now regretted it. For surely this man had demonstrated in the past few minutes that he was perfectly capable of taking care of himself. Even against such men as

Helene might send to accost him? Yes, Lisette believed that might be the case.

That air of easy charm he had affected in the tavern earlier this evening had now been replaced by a narrow-eyed watchfulness. Which Lisette sensed could be as dangerous as Helene's implied threats against him had been such a short time ago. Leading Lisette to believe she had wasted her time, and put herself in danger of incurring Helene's wrath, by leaving the tavern to seek out and warn such a self-assured gentleman.

Her chin rose. 'You were the one waiting outside the tavern in the hope I might join you.'

Christian could hardly argue with the logic of that comment. Unless he also wished to confess to Lisette that she had not been his only reason for skulking about in that doorway tonight.

As he still had no idea yet whether she was the innocent she seemed or an accomplished actress, he would be wiser to allow her to continue with her assumption that his intentions were dishonourable.

Especially as he was unsure if that might not be the case…

Her kiss had seemed to lack experience, but that could have been part of an act. Innocence was not a trait that usually appealed to him in a woman, but it had succeeded in arousing him in Lisette's case.

He was still aroused.

He shifted slightly forward on his seat so that his arousal was not noticeable. 'Are you sorry that I did?' he prompted softly as he took both her gloved hands in his much larger ones and continued to act the *roué* Comte de Saint-Cloud.

She blinked long lashes over those huge blue eyes. 'I—' she moistened plump lips '—I came only to warn you, *mon*—Christian,' she corrected huskily as he gave her a reproving smile.

Christian forced himself not to tense at her comment. 'To warn me of what, *mon ange*?'

It had been so long since anyone had spoken to Lisette with such gentleness, such kindness, that she felt the sting of tears in her eyes.

Helene had provided her with all the necessary comforts—a home, a bed, clothes to wear—but there was no softness in the woman who claimed to have given birth to her. Helene possessed none of the Duprée warmth and easy affection. Indeed, Lisette found it difficult to believe that the older woman could ever have felt passionately enough about a man to have made a child with him.

Until this moment, when the Comte spoke to her so gently, she had been battling so valiantly to adapt to her new life that she had not realised how much she had missed the warmth of another human being.

Even one as dangerously attractive as the Comte de Saint-Cloud.

And he was dangerous. He had flirted with her earlier. Invited her to supper at his home—and goodness knew what else he intended. And he had kissed her a short time ago. A kiss such as Lisette had never imagined receiving from any man. A kiss that had warmed her from her head to her toes, and caused sensations within her body she had never felt before, nor could explain.

She straightened determinedly. 'I came to warn you that Helene is most displeased by the attentions you showed me tonight. So displeased that I believe she might mean to ask some of her...friends to cause you actual physical harm.'

There, she had now done what she intended to do, and given this man fair warning. It was now up to the Comte whether or not he acted upon that warning.

'If you would stop the carriage now?' Lisette requested. 'I believe I might be able to walk back to the tavern from here.' Although she could not say she relished the idea; Helene had warned her that pickpockets—and worse—lurked upon these streets after dark, in search of the unwary and the drink-sodden, and they did not return to their lairs until daybreak. The thought of being accosted by such people as she walked back to the tavern was enough to cause her to tremble.

Christian suspected that there was more about him that 'displeased' Helene Rousseau than his overt flirtation with her young niece.

As for his allowing Lisette to depart his carriage now... 'We will return to my home first, where we can sit and talk in warmth and comfort—'

'Oh, but—'

'If you still wish to return home afterwards—' he talked over what he knew was going to be Lisette's protest '—I will bring you back in my carriage.'

'There is no "if" about it, *monsieur*,' she assured him firmly. 'Nor do I wish to go to your home; an unmarried lady does not enter the house of an unmarried gentleman without causing severe damage to her reputation.'

The fact that Lisette currently lived in a lowly tavern with a woman such as Helene Rousseau was surely already damage enough to her reputation?

As if aware of his thoughts, a blush now appeared in Lisette's cheeks. 'I did not always live in a tavern, *monsieur*,' she informed him stiffly. 'Until just two months ago I lived on a farm in the country with my...with relatives.'

Very curious...

Although it would explain why there had never been any mention of Lisette in the reports made by other agents for the Crown, in connection to Helene or André Rousseau.

'I, for one, am grateful that your aunt brought you to live with her in Paris,' he drawled.

'My aunt?' Lisette repeated sharply.

'Mademoiselle Rousseau,' Christian supplied slowly even as he looked at Lisette searchingly; she seemed surprised—shocked?—by his knowledge of her relationship to the older woman. 'She explained your connection to me earlier this evening,' he added gently.

Lisette moistened her lips with the tip of her tongue. 'Yes, of course…my aunt,' she rallied slightly, even tried to smile a little.

Christian was not fooled for a moment by Lisette's attempt to cover her confusion.

He just had no idea as to the reason for that confusion…

## Chapter Three

Lisette was so taken aback by the Comte de Saint-Cloud's comment regarding her relationship to Helene that she could think of nothing more to add to the conversation.

Of course she accepted that it would have been awkward for Helene to suddenly produce a fully grown daughter.

But surely no more awkward than it was for that fully grown daughter to suddenly discover that the couple she had thought were her parents were not even related to her, and that instead the cold and haughty Helene Rousseau was actually her mother?

Even so, Lisette had not realised until now that Helene had not publicly claimed her as her daughter at all, but instead only as her niece.

She was not sure how she felt about that.

'Lisette…?'

She had been so deeply in thought that she had not realised the carriage had come to a halt, and that a groom now stood beside the open door waiting for her and the Comte to alight.

Which must mean, whilst she had been lost in thought, they had arrived at the Comte de Saint-Cloud's home.

She gave a firm shake of her head. 'I wish to return to the tavern now, *monsieur.*'

'Why?'

'Why? Because…well, because—'

'What so urgently awaits you there, Lisette, that you cannot spare a few minutes to sit and share a glass of wine with me?' the Comte teased softly.

It was not her time that concerned Lisette, but her reputation.

At the same time she felt slightly rebellious after learning that Helene chose to claim her only as her niece—that relationship implying she was the daughter of a man, Helene's brother André, who was now dead.

Also, Lisette did not think that the Comte had taken her at all seriously when she had tried to warn him of the possible danger he was in from Helene Rousseau.

'Very well, *monsieur*, but a few minutes only.' She nodded as she moved forward to step down from the carriage onto the cobbled street, her eyes widening as she looked up at the huge and imposing four-storey house before her. The Comte de Saint-Cloud's Paris home?

Lisette had never seen such a grand house as this, let alone been inside one. She only did so now because the Comte, having ordered the coachman to wait, now took a firm hold of her arm to walk up the steps to the huge front door now being held open by a man dressed in full livery.

The candlelit and cavernous entrance hall took her breath away, with its pale blue walls with gold-inlaid panels, ornate statues and the wide and sweeping staircase to the gallery, a huge crystal chandelier suspended from the high ceiling above.

Lisette felt small, and totally insignificant, amongst such grandeur.

'Brandy and wine in the library, François,' Christian instructed as he handed his coat and cloak to the other man before picking up a candelabrum to light their way through the entrance hall, on his way to the only room in the house he could tolerate for any length of time. The previous owner had possessed an air for the dramatic and ornate in regard to decor, one that did not suit Christian's more elegantly subdued tastes at all.

He could see at a glance that their surroundings had made Lisette shrink back into herself, her face appearing very pale beneath the rim of her black bonnet. Or perhaps that was through nerves at her own temerity in entering the home of a single gentleman? Whichever of those things it was, Christian did not enjoy seeing her so discomfited.

'Sit down in a chair by the fire,' he bade lightly once they had entered the book-lined library, the warmth of a fire crackling in the grate. Hopefully, the heat would bring some colour back into Lisette's cheeks.

'Just for a moment.' Lisette looked so tiny, defenceless, as she sat in the huge wingback armchair, her feet barely touching the ground as she held her gloved hands out towards the flames.

'*Merci*, François, that will be all for tonight.' Christian continued to watch Lisette as he spoke to the other man distractedly, the butler placing the silver tray with the drinks on down onto a side table before departing.

Christian still wondered if Lisette's air of innocence, her reluctance to enter the house with him, could all be an act for his benefit, as he turned his attention to pouring the brandy and wine into two glasses. There was only one way to find out.

But first…

'Your wine, Lisette.' He held the crystal glass out to her.

'*Merci.*'

Christian gave a rueful smile as she took care for her gloved fingers not to come into contact with his own as she took the glass from him.

'What shall we drink to?' he mused. 'Our continued…friendship, perhaps?'

Lisette felt slightly disconcerted by the Comte's close proximity as he made no effort to step away from where she sat after handing her the glass of wine.

He was just so—overpoweringly immediate in these more intimate surroundings. Seemed so much bigger, more imposing even than he had been in the tavern earlier or in his carriage on the journey here.

His shoulders were so wide—and dependable?—his chest and arms muscled beneath the fine cut of his coat, as if he spent much of his time pursuing the gentlemanly sports, such as fencing and swordplay, rather than in the drinking salons, and taverns such as the Fleur de Lis.

His fashionably overlong hair shone a pure gold in the candlelight and was rakishly tousled. As for the effect of those long-lashed lavender-coloured eyes in that harshly handsome and lightly tanned face; Lisette truly had never seen such beautiful eyes before, on a man or a woman.

She was very aware that the two of them were

very much alone here now that he had dismissed his manservant for the night.

Her gaze dropped from meeting that mesmerising lavender one. 'We can drink only to the present, Comte.'

'The present,' he echoed as he gave a mocking inclination of his head before taking a sip of his brandy, 'is very much to my liking,' he added gruffly.

A blush warmed Lisette's cheeks even as she took a sip of her red wine. It was a very good red wine, not at all like the rough vintage Helene served at the tavern. And further emphasising the fact that the Comte de Saint-Cloud inhabited a very different world from the one in which Lisette currently found herself. Even as the daughter of the Duprées she would have been completely out of her element with a man such as this one.

She carefully placed her glass down on the small table beside the chair. 'I do not believe you took my warning seriously earlier, Comte.' She looked up at him earnestly. 'My…my aunt has many associates who are not particularly pleasant, and who I believe would slit your throat for the price of a few pennies if asked to do so.'

'And has your aunt asked them to do so?' Christian arched mocking brows, again noting Lisette's slight hesitation when stating that Helene Rousseau was her aunt. But if not the girl's aunt, then who or what was she to Lisette?

Her madam, perhaps, with Lisette as the innocent prize to be won?

That explanation would certainly be in accordance with Lisette's behaviour tonight. The 'helpless innocent' come to warn him of danger was the sort of behaviour designed to tighten the net about an infatuated victim.

Or Lisette could simply have been sent here to him this evening in order to confirm or deny, by whatever means necessary, Helene Rousseau's suspicions regarding him.

'I believe she has, yes,' Lisette answered him worriedly.

'And why do you think that?' Christian moved to sit in the chair opposite her, his posture one of outward relaxation and unconcern; inwardly it was a different matter.

The title of Comte de Saint-Cloud might be his own to use if he so wished, but nevertheless he was alone in a country that was not his own and amongst people he could not trust.

Not even the lovely Lisette.

Perhaps especially the lovely Lisette.

'She assured me earlier that I would not be seeing you at the tavern again after this evening.' Lisette frowned.

Christian raised his brows. 'That was very… precipitate of her.'

'I believe it was because she already has plans afoot to ensure you are unable to return, *monsieur*,' Lisette pressed urgently.

'Christian.'

She gave him an impatient glance. 'What does it matter in what manner I address you, if you are not alive to hear it?'

Christian gave a lazy smile. 'I am not that easy to kill, lovely Lisette. Besides,' he continued lightly as she would have protested, 'I am alive here and now, and we are together, which is all that is important, is it not?'

'No, it most certainly is not all that is important!' She eyed him exasperatedly.

'I find your concern for me most charming,
Lisette,' he drawled flirtatiously. 'But you really
need not concern yourself on my account—'

'How can I not concern myself?' She rose
agitatedly to her feet. 'When I am the reason
you are in danger?'

Christian sincerely doubted that; he was becoming more and more convinced by the moment that Helene Rousseau did suspect him and
his reason for being in Paris. To a degree where
it was no longer safe for him to continue to remain here posing as the Comte de Saint-Cloud'.

That would be a pity, considering all the work
and planning that had gone into establishing that
identity before his arrival in France.

It also meant that tonight might be the only
time he had left in Paris.

A night he might spend with Lisette?

He placed his brandy glass down on the side
table before rising lazily to his feet. 'I am sure
you would feel more comfortable if you were to
remove your bonnet and cloak.'

'I do not wish to feel more comfortable—'

'Of course you do.' Christian crossed the distance that separated them before unfastening her bonnet himself and removing it, ignoring her efforts to stop him as he then untied the cloak at her throat before placing them both down on the armchair and turning back to her. 'Much better,' he noted with satisfaction as he took both of her gloved hands in one of his.

He did not particularly care for the plain black gown Lisette was wearing, would much rather see her in bright colours that would flatter rather than detract from her delicate complexion. But her hair gleamed like copper in the firelight, and the warmth of the fire had indeed brought back a little of the colour to her cheeks.

She looked slightly bewildered at his deft removal of her bonnet and cloak. 'I told you I cannot stay above a minute or two—'

'You really must not distress yourself, my dear Lisette,' Christian soothed softly. 'As I have said, we have tonight together...' He held her now startled gaze as he slowly lowered his head towards her.

Lisette's head began to spin as she knew thi completely compelling man, Christian Beau mont, Comte de Saint-Cloud, was about to kiss her again.

She couldn't move, was held completely mes merised by those lavender eyes gazing down into her own as the Comte's lips brushed gently against hers.

Her hands were still held captive in his much larger one as his other arm moved about her waist and pulled her in tightly against him. In stantly making Lisette aware of his strength and the hardness of his muscled chest.

Until tonight she had never been kissed before but she was sure that if she had it would not have made her feel the way that Christian's kisses did as if she were floating on air and Christian's arm about her waist was the only thing keeping her feet on the ground.

Her life had been so miserable since coming to Paris, everything strange and uncomfortable to her, and this—being held by Christian, being kissed by him—was so overwhelmingly *plea surable* after so many weeks of unhappiness and uncertainty and feeling that she no longer belonged anywhere.

For this moment, for here and for now, surely she could just forget all of that and enjoy being in this man's arms.

Lisette pulled her hands free of his to glide them up the length of his muscled chest before resting them on his shoulders, as she stood on tiptoe and returned the kiss. Not expertly, she was sure, but she hoped that what she lacked in experience she more than made up for in her obvious enjoyment and enthusiasm.

Better—much, much better, Christian acknowledged with inner satisfaction as he deepened the kiss by running his tongue lightly, questioningly, along the line of Lisette's closed lips. He felt her brief hesitation before those softly pouting lips parted, allowing him access as his tongue now glided inside the moist and welcoming heat of her mouth.

He groaned softly as he felt the stroke of her tongue along his, hesitant at first and then more assuredly. His body instantly responded to the intimacy, engorging, and lengthening impatiently inside his pantaloons.

Christian pressed his body intimately into Lisette's as he kissed her harder, deeper. Hearing her responding groan as his tongue now explored the sweetness of her mouth, at the same time as his hands moved restlessly up and down the length of her spine.

His fingers brushed against the tiny buttons fastening the back of her gown, and he continued to kiss her as he unfastened enough of those buttons to slip one of his hands inside and touch the softness of her bare skin.

She felt like silk beneath his fingertips. Warm, soft silk that seemed to heat to the touch of his caressing hands.

It was not enough. Christian needed to see all of her. To touch her. To caress and pleasure her—

*'No!'* Lisette had wrenched her mouth away from Christian's to protest, eyes wide as she stared up at him in what looked like a mixture of fascination and shock.

The first emotion Christian could understand;

he was experienced enough to know when a woman found pleasure in his kisses. And he had no doubt Lisette had enjoyed their kisses as much as he had.

The shock appeared to have occurred because he had unfastened her gown and touched her bared skin…

Her dilated pupils, and the quick rise and fall of her breasts as she breathed deeply, told him that Lisette's shock was completely genuine.

Not a whore, then.

The mystery that surrounded this young woman deepened every second they were together.

She pushed determinedly against his chest now in an effort to escape his imprisoning arms. 'You must release me, Christian. Please!' Her eyes met his in appeal when her efforts to free herself proved unsuccessful.

He looked down at her searchingly. 'You did not enjoy being kissed?'

'No! Well. Yes.' A blush heated her cheeks. 'Of course I enjoyed being kissed—'

'Then why have you stopped me?'

*Why had she stopped him?*

For the same reason she knew that she could not remain here alone in this room with this man a moment longer.

Because she had enjoyed his kisses too much. Had wanted his hands upon her bared flesh too much.

*Because she had wanted so much more than just his kisses.*

For just a brief time, a few moments, Lisette had wanted to lose herself in Christian's kisses and caresses, to forget the unhappiness of these past months, along with the uncertainty of no longer knowing who or what she was.

For this time, here with Christian, she had wanted to just be herself. The Lisette Duprée who had been loved and cherished by the couple she had believed were her parents, and not the illegitimate daughter of a woman who seemed to care nothing for her, who owned and ran a lowly Parisian tavern frequented by criminals and whores.

That same woman who Lisette now knew had not even claimed her as being her daughter.

Except it really would not do.

The brief pleasure Lisette might know in Christian Beaumont's arms would not, could not, drive away the otherwise unhappiness of her life for more than a few minutes, at the most hours.

Whereas the reality of the life she now led would last for her lifetime.

'I have to go.' She avoided meeting Christian's gaze as she stepped away from him. 'I must return to the tavern before I am missed—'

'Perhaps you have already been missed…?'

Her heart leaped apprehensively in her chest. 'Do not say that, Christian, even in jest.'

Christian frowned. He saw how pale her face was in the firelight. 'Do you fear retribution from your aunt?'

'No.' Her gaze avoided meeting his. 'No, of course I do not.'

Her denial came too quickly for Christian's liking. 'Come away with me, Lisette.' The offer was completely spontaneous and as much of a surprise to Christian as it appeared to be to Lisette. 'We could go to my country estate—'

the Saint-Cloud family still had one somewhere in Brittany '—or…the war is over now and I have relatives in England. I could take you there if you would rather leave France altogether?'

'Leave France?' she echoed faintly, as if the idea both thrilled and terrified her.

Christian regretted his offer as soon as the words left his mouth. The idea of taking Lisette back to England with him was ridiculous; what would he possibly do with the niece of Helene Rousseau once they were back in England?

For one thing, once in England, Lisette would quickly realise that he was not Christian Beaumont, the Comte de Saint-Cloud, at all, but in actual fact Christian Seaton, the Duke of Sutherland.

But perhaps, as he suspected in regard to her aunt, Lisette already knew that, and returning to England with him had been her plan all along?

Admittedly, she had looked shocked at the idea, but Christian still had no proof, either way, whether Lisette was all that she seemed to be.

Indeed, he was more unsure than ever as to what she *seemed*.

The niece Helene Rousseau claimed her to be? A description which had seemed to startle Lisette when he'd called her such earlier.

Or something else completely?

No doubt Lord Aubrey Maystone, his immediate superior in his work for the Crown, would be more than happy to have the niece of Helene Rousseau in his clutches, after the kidnapping of his young grandson.

What might happen to Lisette once Christian had delivered her into the older man's hands did not bear thinking about; Christian's first loyalty might be to the Crown, but he had no evidence that Lisette was guilty of anything, other than the misfortune of being related to Helene Rousseau. Which would make her an innocent pawn, as Aubrey Maystone's grandson had been.

It was not a risk Christian was willing to take.

'A ridiculous idea, is it not, when I have only just arrived in Paris and there is still so much for me to enjoy?' he dismissed lightly.

Lisette blinked at the Comte's about-turn when, just for a moment, a brief euphoric moment, she had dreamed of escaping Paris, the tavern and her association with Helene Rousseau. To leave France completely and begin again somewhere new, where no one knew her or the shameful secret of her birth she carried with her every moment of every day.

But the Comte was perfectly correct; it would not do, and it was ridiculous of her to have even contemplated the possibility.

She frowned up at him. 'It is your intention to remain in Paris, even after the things I have told you?'

The Comte gave an indifferent shrug. 'I thank you for your concern, of course. But I am sure your worries are unfounded and Madame Rousseau will have forgotten all about my flirtation with you by tomorrow.'

Lisette wished she could feel as confident of that. Unfortunately, she could not.

But she had done what she intended tonight, and if the Comte would not take her warning seriously, then there was nothing more she could do. 'If I might prevail upon your generosity for the use of your carriage to take me back to the Fleur de Lis?' She really could not bear the thought of travelling back by foot along the streets to the tavern.

'But of course.' The Comte gave a charming bow. 'I will accompany you, of course—'

'I would rather you did not.' Lisette replaced and retied her bonnet before reaching for her cloak. 'I will instruct your coachman to stop a street or two away from the tavern and make my own way back from there.'

Christian scowled his displeasure. 'That is too dangerous—'

'Nevertheless, it is what I shall do,' she stated determinedly.

Not what she 'intended' to do, Christian noted with wry amusement, but what she would do. Lisette Duprée might be young in years, but she had a very determined and definite mind of her own.

No more so than he, admittedly, and if she thought he really intended to allow her to walk the Paris streets alone at this time of night, even for a short distance, then she was mistaken.

'It is far too early for me to retire as yet,' he informed her airily. 'I can see you safely returned to the tavern on my way to other entertainments.'

Lisette looked up from refastening her cloak. 'You are going out again…?'

'But of course.' The Comte waved a hand unconcernedly. 'The gaming hells and…other clubs will only now be becoming interesting.'

Of course they would, Lisette acknowledged heavily. And no doubt the Comte would be luckier with the ladies in those clubs, as well as the cards, now that she had refused to entertain him for the rest of the night.

She had behaved the fool, she realised. A stupid, naive fool, to have believed for one moment that the Comte had any more than a passing interest in her—an interest that had obviously 'passed' now that she had made it clear she did not intend to spend the night here with him.

She raised her chin. 'I am ready to leave now.'

Christian knew by the stiffness of Lisette's demeanour that he had thoroughly succeeded in alienating her when he'd informed her that he intended to go out again. As had been his intention. His mission in Paris had been clear:

to watch Helene Rousseau and make note of the comings and goings of the Fleur de Lis.

It had occurred to him earlier to use an interest in one of the tavern's serving girls to enable him to observe Helene Rousseau and the movements of her co-conspirators. Unfortunately, his choice of Lisette as the focus for that interest seemed only to have antagonised the older woman, so bringing more attention to himself.

Helene Rousseau's threats towards him, because of the interest he had shown in Lisette, now meant that his time in Paris was in all probability limited, if he did not want to end up dead in a filthy alley one night.

## Chapter Four

'Where have you been?'

Lisette, having just closed and locked the window behind her, after climbing back into the storeroom at the back of the tavern, now gave a gasp of shock as she turned to face her accuser.

Helene stood in the doorway in her night robe, her tall frame silhouetted by the candle left burning outside in the hallway, her hair loose about her shoulders, eyes glittering with her displeasure. 'I asked where you have been,' she repeated harshly.

Lisette swallowed, her lips having gone dry. 'I could not sleep— I went— I thought to—' She faltered as she realised that nothing she said was going to excuse the fact that she had obviously left the tavern sometime earlier tonight and was now sneaking back in again. Or change the fact that Helene had somehow discovered her disappearance. 'I went for a walk.' Her chin rose in challenge.

Helene reached for the candle in the hallway, bringing the light into the room to illuminate the stored barrels and sacks, as well as a defiant and no doubt dishevelled Lisette; how could she be any other when she had been climbing in and out of a window?

'You went to Saint-Cloud.' Helene's nostrils flared with distaste. 'Do not attempt to deny it; I saw you arrive back just now in his carriage.'

Lisette's heart sank. She had told Monsieur le Comte, had in fact pleaded with him to let her depart the carriage in the street adjoining this one, but he would have none of it. Had instead insisted on bringing her to the back door of the tavern and waiting in his carriage until he was sure she had climbed safely back inside. She had seen his carriage depart as she closed and locked the window.

Well, the Comte was now gone, she was 'back

inside', but the fury in Helene's expression did not augur well for it being 'safely'.

Helene carefully placed the lit candle down on top of one of the barrels. 'I told you earlier that I did not approve of you associating any further with the Comte.'

'I do not believe you actually told me not to—'

'Do not contradict me, Lisette.' The woman who was her mother glared at her furiously. 'The Comte is a dangerous man.'

'He has always behaved the gentleman towards me,' Lisette defended, her cheeks burning as she knew that was not strictly true; after all, he had kissed her, not once, but twice.

Helene gave an impatient shake of her head at that telling blush. 'You have not only openly defied me by meeting secretly with the Comte, but defiled your own reputation at the same time—'

'I have done nothing wrong!' she asserted heatedly.

'I do not believe you.'

'I do not care—' She broke off with a pained gasp as Helene's hand struck out at her face. Hard.

Lisette raised a shocked hand as she felt the

sting of pain and then the flow of blood on her bottom lip, her fingers covered with the sticky redness when she looked down at them through tear-filled eyes.

No one had ever struck her before this. Not for any reason.

She kept her hand pressed against her bleeding lip as she glared her defiance at the older woman. 'That was truly unforgivable!'

'No more so than your own behaviour has been tonight.' Helene looked at her coldly, unrepentantly. 'I did not bring you to Paris so that you could whore yourself for the first titled gentleman to show you attention.'

'Then why did you bring me here?' Lisette challenged, chin held high. 'You do not care for me. You do not even acknowledge me as your daughter,' she added scornfully as she remembered what the Comte had said to her earlier. 'What am I even doing here?'

Helene gave a snort. 'What else was I supposed to do with you once I learned the Duprées were both dead?'

Lisette felt a fresh sting of tears in her eyes at this woman's total lack of feeling for her.

If she had needed any confirmation of that, after Helene had just struck her without warning or sign of regret.

She straightened her spine. 'In that case, it will be no hardship to you if I remove myself from here tomorrow.'

'To go where?' the older woman derided. 'To your titled lover, perhaps? As if the Comte would have you! To a man such as he, you will either have been no more than a source of information about me—'

'You flatter yourself, *madame*!'

'—or a willing female body in his bed. If it was the latter, then I have no doubt he has already forgotten you!'

Lisette could not deny the truth of this last comment; that the Comte had gone out for further entertainment, after bringing her back to the tavern, proved that the kisses they had shared had meant nothing to him. As she meant nothing to him.

'Do not assume everyone to have the same

morals as yourself, *madame*,' she hit back in her humiliation.

'Why, you little—'

'If you hit me again, then I shall be forced to retaliate!' Lisette warned, her hands now clenched into fists at her sides as she faced the taller woman challengingly.

Helene fell back a step as grudging respect dawned in those icy blue eyes. 'This is the first occasion when I have seen any visible sign that you are my daughter.'

'And it will be the last!' Lisette assured her scornfully. 'I intend to pack my bags, such as they are, and leave here in the morning.'

'As I asked before—to go where?' The older woman looked at her coldly. 'You have only the few francs I have given you since you arrived here; have no other money of your own. You do not own anything that I have not given you. You *have* nowhere else to go, Lisette.'

Another indisputable truth.

The very same truth Lisette had told Christian Beaumont earlier this evening…

'If you choose to leave here, you will have no

choice but to become a whore or to starve,' Helene added cruelly.

'Then I will starve, *madame*,' she replied with dignity.

'You are behaving like a child, Lisette,' the other woman bit out impatiently.

No, what Lisette was doing inwardly was shaking in reaction to this unpleasant conversation, and her bottom lip now felt sore and swollen from the painful slap she had received from Helene Rousseau. Something Lisette still found difficult to believe had happened at all, when the Duprées, of no relationship to her at all, had shown her nothing but love and kindness for the past nineteen years.

Although that slap certainly made it easier for Lisette to accept her own lack of softer feelings towards Helene. Something she had felt guilty about until this moment. But no longer. Helene Rousseau was a cold and unemotional woman, and one Lisette found it impossible to feel affection for, let alone love. Now that she had decided to leave she did not need to bother trying to do that any more.

Helene was right, of course, in that Lisette did not have anywhere else to go, nor did she have more than a few francs to her name, but her pride dictated she could not allow that to sway her in her decision. She did not belong here. Not in the sprawling city that was Paris. And definitely not in this lowly tavern.

'But not *your* child,' she came back scornfully. 'You do not claim me as such, nor do you have any right to do so after your behaviour tonight,' she added as the other woman would have spoken. 'If you permit it, I will stay here for what is left of the night and leave first thing in the morning.' She gathered her cloak protectively about her.

Helene sighed wearily. 'Lisette…'

'Did you even bother to name me yourself before handing me over to the Duprées?' Lisette challenged derisively. 'Or did you leave even the naming of your child to strangers?' She knew by the angry flush that appeared in the older woman's cheeks that it had been the latter.

'Surely you realise I could not have kept you here with me, Lisette—'

'Could not? Or maybe you did not want to tarnish what is left of your own reputation by acknowledging me as your bastard child?'

Helene sighed heavily. 'It is far too late at night for this conversation—'

'It is too late altogether, *madame*.' Lisette gave a disgusted shake of her head. 'Would that you had left me in ignorance in the country.'

'To do what? Live off turnips and marry a local peasant?' The older woman's lip curled.

'Far better I had done that than live in this place!' Lisette retorted. 'I will leave here as soon as I am able,' she repeated wearily as she brushed past the other woman to gather up a candle and light it before walking proudly down the hallway and going up the stairs.

She made it all the way to her bedchamber before giving in to the tears that had been threatening to fall since she had received that slap on her face.

Tears that were long overdue, as she placed the candle carefully on the bedside table before throwing herself down on the bed and sobbing in earnest; for the loss of the Duprées and the life she had known with them, for the shock of discovering Helene Rousseau was her mother, for her unhappiness since coming to Paris, for the lack of prospects ahead of her once she had left this place.

For the knowledge that the lavender-eyed Comte *had* in all probability already forgotten her existence.

Christian had instructed his coachman to drive around and park the carriage a short distance from the front entrance of the Fleur de Lis, once he was assured Lisette had climbed safely into one of the downstairs windows of the tavern. He was determined, before leaving the area completely, to see that Lisette reached her bedchamber safely.

He had been lying, of course, when he told Lisette he intended to go on to further entertainment. Helene Rousseau, and the clandestine comings and goings to her tavern, was his only reason for being in Paris.

At least it had been.

The puzzle that was Lisette Duprée had changed that somewhat.

There was a mystery there he did not understand. Helene Rousseau had been so overprotective of Lisette earlier in the tavern when she held a gun to his back, and yet at the same time there was an obvious lack of familial feeling between the two women. A disconnection that surely should not have been there—

Ah, he had just seen candlelight behind the curtains in the bedchamber he believed to be Lisette's, instantly reassuring him as to her safe return.

'Drive on,' Christian instructed his coachman before settling back against the plush upholstery, his mind still occupied with the relationship between Helene Rousseau and Lisette.

There had never been mention of André Rousseau having a daughter, and surely the other man could not have been old enough to have a daughter of Lisette's age? And yet, to Christian's knowledge, Helene Rousseau had no other siblings.

In any case, the discovery of Lisette was an

unexpected vulnerability in regard to Helene Rousseau. One that Christian felt sure Aubrey Maystone would not hesitate to use against that lady. As the Frenchwoman had been involved in using other innocents as pawns in her own wicked games.

Christian frowned at the very idea of using Lisette in that way.

Another reason for not taking her back to England with him?

He found the whole concept of using her as a pawn in a game to be totally repugnant. Complete anathema to his code as a gentleman.

And yet there was no place for a gentlemanly code when it came to the defence of the Crown.

But to use Lisette in that way, no matter whether she was the innocent she appeared to be or something more, did not sit well with Christian—

'We have company, milord!' his coachman had time to call out grimly seconds before the carriage came to a lurching halt and the door beside Christian was wrenched open, a masked man appearing in that open doorway, a raised pistol in his hand.

Lisette's earlier warning barely had time to register before there was a flash in the darkness and the sound of a pistol being fired.

Lisette sat up with a start, her tears ceasing as she heard the sound of an explosion of some kind ringing through the stillness of the night, followed by the sound of raised voices.

She rose quickly to her feet before hurrying across the bedchamber to look out of the window.

The street was poorly lit, of course, but she could see a carriage a short way down, and it appeared to be surrounded by a group of darkly clothed men. A carriage that seemed all too familiar to her, considering she had been driven back to the tavern in it just a short time ago.

The Comte de Saint-Cloud's carriage!

Lisette gave no thought to her own safety as she ran across the bedchamber and threw open the door before running down the hallway to descend the stairs. She heard the sound of a second shot being fired and then a third, causing her fingers to fumble with the bolts and key as she quickly unlocked the front door of the tavern before throwing it open and running out into the street.

The carriage was still parked a short distance away, but there were no longer any dark-clothed men surrounding it, the street quiet apart from the horses snorting and stamping their shod feet on the cobbled road in their obvious distress.

Lisette stilled her mad flight at the sound of that deathly silence, her steps becoming hesitant as she approached the carriage, its door flung open and swinging slightly in the breeze.

In keeping with this lowly neighbourhood, no one else had emerged from any of the buildings in response to hearing those three shots being fired, and Lisette herself feared what she might find once she had reached and looked inside that eerily silent carriage.

She raised a shocked hand to her mouth as she drew nearer and saw a body lying on the cobbles beside the carriage, recognising the groom who had opened the door for her earlier tonight lying so still and unmoving, a bloom of red having appeared on the chest of his grey livery.

Which surely meant that the Comte de Saint-Cloud was inside the carriage still; otherwise Lisette had no doubt he would be out here now tending to his groom. Or perhaps, having discovered the man dead, he was off chasing the men who had attacked them.

She ceased breathing and her heart seemed to stop beating altogether as she apprehensively approached the open door of the carriage, so very afraid of what she was going to find when she looked inside.

In all possibility, the Comte, as dead as his groom appeared to be?

Her heart stuttered and then stopped again as she heard the sound of a groan from inside the depths of the carriage. Indication that at least the Comte was alive, if obviously injured?

'Christian!' Lisette called out frantically as she no longer hesitated but hurriedly ascended the steps.

'Lisette?' The Comte groaned uncomprehendingly, the lantern inside the carriage showing him lying back against the cushions, his face deathly white, a bloom of red showing, and growing larger by the second, on the left thigh of his pale-coloured pantaloons. 'You should not be here,' he protested as he attempted to sit up.

'Do not move!' Lisette instructed sternly as she stepped fully into the carriage to fall to her knees beside him and began to inspect the wound to his thigh.

'They might come back—'

'I doubt it,' she snorted disgustedly. 'Cowards. Half a dozen men against two—'

'You saw them?' Christian, grateful that he had the foresight to speak to Lisette in French, had now managed to ease himself back into an upright position, although his thigh hurt like the very devil with every movement.

Lisette nodded distractedly, her face a pale oval in the lamplight. 'From the window of my bedchamber. At least half a dozen men. Are you hurt very badly?' She looked at his thigh but did not attempt to touch him.

Christian's jaw was clenched against the pain.

'I believe the bullet has gone through the soft tissue and out the other side.'

Lisette's face seemed to pale even more. 'We should call for law enforcement, and you need a doctor—'

'No—no doctor,' he refused grimly.

'You are bleeding badly—'

'No, Lisette,' he repeated determinedly. 'My groom?'

Her gaze dropped from meeting his. 'I fear— He does not appear to be—'

'Damn it, they have killed him!' Christian struggled to sit forward, intent on seeing his groom for himself. 'Please move aside, Lisette, so that I can go to him.'

'You must not move, Christian—'

'Indeed I must, Lisette.' He gritted his teeth as that movement caused his leg to throb and the blood to flow more freely over the fingers he had pressed to his flesh to staunch the wound. He looked at Lisette as she now sat on the other side of the carriage, a bewildered look upon her face. 'I am afraid I shall need your help to get Pierre into the carriage.'

Her face lost any remaining colour at the mere idea of touching a dead body. Christian nodded approvingly as she nonetheless moved valiantly forward to follow as he stepped awkwardly down from the carriage, before limping over and going down on one knee beside his groom lying un-moving on the cobbles.

'Not dead, and I think the shot has pierced his shoulder rather than his chest,' Christian said thankfully after placing his bloody fin-gers against the other man's wrist and feeling a pulse. 'Help me lift him inside the carriage, would you?'

'I— But— What are you going to do with him then?'

'Return to my home, of course.'

Lisette felt totally perplexed by the Comte's behaviour. Surely a doctor, at least, should be called for, even if Christian did not feel inclined to ask for the help of the police enforcement that had been established in Paris just five years ago.

The dissolute rake he had appeared earlier this evening was completely gone, Christian Beau-mont's eyes now sharp with intelligence and determination as the two of them struggled to lift the groom and place him inside the carriage.

Not an easy task when the Comte was injured and Lisette was so slight in stature.

It seemed to take forever as they struggled to get Pierre inside the carriage and lying on one of the bench seats, but was in fact probably only a few minutes. Both of them were smeared with the other man's blood by that time, and Christian Beaumont's own wound seemed to be bleeding more profusely too.

Lisette gave a dismayed gasp at how deathly pale his face was as he straightened. 'I really must insist you are attended by a doctor—'

'I shall consider it once we are returned to my home and I have been able to inspect Pierre's wound more thoroughly.' He nodded grimly even as he placed a hand against the carriage for support.

Lisette frowned her disapproval. 'And exactly how do you intend doing that, when both your groom and yourself have been shot?'

A touch of humour tilted the Comte's lips. 'Di

you ever drive a horse and cart on that farm you once lived on, Lisette?'

She gave him a startled look. 'You are not suggesting that *I* should drive your carriage...?'

He gave a pointed look about the empty street. 'I do not see anyone else I can ask, do you?'

'But— Christian!' Lisette stepped forward to put her arm about the leanness of his waist and the support of her shoulder beneath his arm as he appeared to sway precariously.

'And I suggest that you do it soon, Lisette,' he muttered faintly. 'Whilst I am still conscious to direct you.'

She had never heard of anything so ridiculous as to expect her to drive the Comte's carriage; it was nothing like the old cart they'd had on the farm, nor were the four horses pulling this elegant carriage in the least like the elderly and plodding mare owned by the Duprées. Indeed, these high-stepping animals might have been a different breed altogether from the docile Marguerite.

Lisette eyed the four black horses doubtfully as they still snorted and stamped their displeasure. 'You are asking too much, Christian.' She gave a shake of her head.

He nodded. 'I would not ask at all if it were not important.'

Lisette looked up at him searchingly. 'I do not understand,' she finally murmured slowly.

'And I do not have the time, or indeed the strength, to explain the situation to you right now.' He sighed weakly.

Lisette glanced down to where his thigh was still bleeding freely, front and back. 'Something needs to be tied about your thigh in order to slow the bleeding...'

'Lisette...?' Christian's eyes widened as she did not hesitate to lift her gown before efficiently ripping a strip from the bottom of her petticoat and then proceeded to crouch down in front of him to wrap and tie that strip tightly about the top of his thigh.

It was perhaps as well that there was no one on the street to observe them because Lisette crouched in that position, looked very—risqué if one did not realise she was merely applying a tourniquet to his thigh.

'There.' She gave a nod of satisfaction as she straightened, seemingly completely unaware of the picture of debauchery she had just presented to the world. 'I shall need your instruction to drive the carriage, Christian. Do you feel strong enough to be helped up into the driving area?'

He determinedly dragged his thoughts back from the lewdly suggestive delights that having Lisette kneeling in front of him had evoked.

It looked a very long way up to where his groom drove the carriage, when he was feeling less than agile, the loss of blood having also made him feel slightly light-headed.

He set his jaw grimly. 'I shall manage with your help, yes.' He was determined to do so, knew that he and Lisette must now get themselves away from here as soon as was possible, that they had delayed long enough.

He had no doubt that the men who had accosted and then shot him and Pierre were the cut-throats Lisette had warned him Helene Rousseau had intended sending to dispose of him. That at any moment they might return and finish the job.

There was no sign of life or candlelight inside the Fleur de Lis itself, but that did not mean that Helene Rousseau was not observing the two of them right now. And no doubt filled with fresh resolve now that she had seen he was not only still alive but also mobile enough to struggle up onto the carriage with Lisette's help.

That resolve would no doubt deepen, and Helene Rousseau herself be filled with renewed rage, when she saw her niece drive away with him in his carriage.

'Perhaps you should not accompany me, after all.' Christian frowned as Lisette climbed up beside him. 'Your aunt will no doubt make her disapproval known—'

'I have already told Helene that I shall be leaving the Fleur de Lis in the morning.' She shrugged.

'The two of you have argued?'

'That is one way of describing it.' Lisette's hand moved up to touch her mouth.

Christian's eyes darkened as he saw her bottom lip was slightly swollen. 'She struck you?'

'Yes.'

'Because of me?'

'The reason is unimportant.' Her expression was grim as she picked up the reins, ready for departing. 'And she is not my aunt.'

'Not your aunt…?' Christian echoed softly, the effort of climbing up into the carriage having taken the last of his strength.

'No.' Lisette's jaw was clenched.

Well, that at least explained Lisette's hesitation every time he referred to her as such. It did not, however—

'Madame Rousseau is my mother, not my aunt,' she continued scathingly. 'And I do not care what her opinion might be on any of my actions after the way she has behaved this night!'

Christian dropped back weakly against the seat, knowing that this revelation now gave him no choice where Lisette was concerned.

Leaving Helene Rousseau's niece behind in Paris might have been explained away—just— but the daughter of Helene Rousseau *must* return with him to England.

## Chapter Five

The journey was a long and painful one, as each rumble of the carriage wheels over the cobbled streets caused renewed pain to spear up through Christian's thigh, and it took every effort of will on his part to stay conscious long enough to direct Lisette in the initial driving of the carriage. Luckily, she was an intelligent as well as capable young lady, and had mastered the horses and the carriage within a few minutes.

Leaving Christian to contemplate the leaden weight in his chest at the knowledge that the young woman sitting beside him was the daughter of a woman believed responsible for attempting to free the Corsican usurper by causing actual physical harm to people he cared about.

A belief Christian was even more convinced

of after the attack on him tonight. An attack Lisette believed to have happened because of his attentions towards her earlier this evening, but which Christian believed to have been for a different reason entirely; Helene Rousseau not only knew *who* he was, but also the reason for his currently being in Paris.

And if she knew that, then there was every chance that she would try to have him killed a second time, if he remained here. More than a chance, now that he had her daughter with him.

Once returned to his temporary home he would have to make immediate arrangements for both himself and Lisette to take ship to England. Without, he acknowledged heavily, telling Lisette exactly why he was taking her with him. He doubted she would come with him to England at all if she knew who he was and the reason he had been in Paris, much less that he now had no choice but to deliver Helene Rousseau's daughter to Aubrey Maystone.

No, much as it pained him, he could not tell Lisette any of those things just yet.

Better by far that he at least waited until they

were on the ship bound for England, when it was too late for Lisette to do anything else but complete the voyage. That she would dislike him intensely afterwards could not be avoided.

Lisette had been keeping half an eye on the Comte as she carefully guided the carriage through the deserted Paris streets, and so she knew the exact moment that he lost consciousness. Either from loss of too much blood or from the pain he was suffering. The latter, she hoped, otherwise there was a serious possibility that he might die before she was able to get him to help.

A part of her still wanted to take him to the home of the nearest doctor—if she had known where that was, which she did not—but the Comte had been adamant in his refusal of medical assistance, and Lisette did not wish to make this situation any worse than it already was by going against his wishes.

If that was possible.

At the moment she had two unconscious men in the carriage with her, one seated beside her, the other inside the carriage. Both of them clearly suffering wounds from a pistol shot. And she herself was covered in blood from both those gentlemen, on her hands and her gown. If she was stopped by the authorities—

Hysteria could come later, Lisette told herself sternly. Once they had safely reached the Comte's home. She did not have the time or thought enough to spare for such things when she was so concentrated on driving the Comte's carriage.

She breathed a sigh of relief when she recognised the Comte's house just a short distance away, her shoulders and back aching from controlling such spirited horses, and her hands sore from grasping the reins so tightly.

She almost cried with relief when she finally drew the carriage to a halt in front of the house, François's politely bland expression as he opened the door changing to one of alarm as he ran down the steps to grab hold of the bridle of one of the front horses.

'The Comte and his groom have both been shot, François,' Lisette explained economically as she hitched up the skirt of her gown to quickly climb down from the carriage.

It was testament to the man's character that he wasted no time asking for explanations but instead instantly called up to a hovering footman for reinforcements. Several other footmen now appeared from inside the house, followed by a couple of grooms from the back of the house.

Between them they managed to lift the still unconscious Comte and the groom from the carriage before carrying them inside. Lisette insisted that the groom must also be carried up to one of the guest bedchambers. If Christian would not allow a doctor to be called for, then she would have to do the best she could to doctor the two men herself, and it would be far easier for her if they were within feet of each other.

Again, François showed his character by not so much as batting an eyelid at her request, but instead continued the directing of the two wounded men after sending one of the footmen off to the kitchen to acquire the supplies Lisette said she would need to clean and then dress their wounds.

If either man still had a bullet inside one of those wounds then she would have no choice but to send for a doctor, despite Christian's instructions to the contrary. A bullet, left inside the wound, would surely fill with pus and possibly result in the man dying.

There was no doubt in Lisette's mind that if he were awake Christian would have insisted she attend to the groom first, but as he was not…

François proved to be her rock during the next hour, helping her to remove the Comte's boots, pantaloons and undergarments—a moment when Lisette had discreetly looked the other way—and acting as her assistant as she inspected and then cleaned both the entry and exit wounds in Christian's thigh; he was proved correct, in that the bullet had gone straight through the soft tissue of his thigh and then out again.

Nevertheless, once her makeshift tourniquet had been removed both wounds bled profusely and she was grateful that Christian continued to remain unconscious throughout. He looked so pale and still once she had bound his wound tightly to allow the skin to knit back together— he should perhaps have had stitches applied, but again Lisette did not feel qualified to do so, and so they had just made him as comfortable as they could beneath the bedclothes once she had applied the bandages.

Which was when the enormity of what she had just done bore down upon Lisette. Not only had she dressed the Comte's bloody wounds, but he had been half-naked as she did so. Admittedly François had draped the sheet across Christian's groin to protect his modesty, but that did not alter the fact that he had been completely naked beneath that sheet.

'Would you care for some brandy before we go to Pierre, *mademoiselle*?' François offered as he looked at her concernedly.

She smiled her gratitude for that concern. 'Perhaps afterwards, thank you, François. It would perhaps be as well if I continue to have a steady hand until after I have seen to Pierre!' she added ruefully.

François was the one to once again undress the man lying injured on the bed while they waited for one of the footmen to bring up fresh hot water and bandages. Allowing them to see that the groom's wound was in the shoulder, as

Christian had surmised it might be, but more complicated, in that the bullet was obviously still embedded in his flesh.

'It will have to come out, *mademoiselle*,' François said with a frown.

Lisette swayed slightly on her feet, both from the gory work of this past hour and the deep fatigue she felt after such a long and exhausting day.

It seemed far longer than the six, or possibly seven, hours since she had first met the Comte de Saint-Cloud at the Fleur de Lis. Six or seven hours when her life had been completely turned about, to the point that she now had no home, and no family to speak of.

Self-pity was not permissible now, Lisette told herself firmly, any more than it had been when the Duprées both perished. She might not have a home or a family, but the Comte had been shot because of his association with her, and the outcome of his wound was still questionable.

As was poor Pierre's...

She straightened her shoulders determinedly. 'I will need something with which to remove the bullet, François. And your assistance for a little longer, if you please.'

'As long as it takes, *mademoiselle*,' he assured her gravely.

Lisette gave him a grateful smile before she turned her attention to the now ashen-faced groom.

Christian awakened with a groan of pain, feeling as if he had been kicked by a horse and then his leg trampled upon by that same horse.

Every part of him seemed to hurt, but it pained him the most in his left thigh. He had no idea—

'Do not attempt to move, Your Grace,' a voice advised urgently in English.

Christian had no strength to struggle against the hand now pressing against his shoulder, and so instead he opened heavy lids to look up at a dishevelled François, the weak sunlight shining in through the window of his bedchamber showing him that the man's coat was unfastened over a bloody shirt, his wig slightly askew on his bald head, and there were dark shadows under his eyes. A testament to lack of sleep?

'I believe we must keep to Monsieur le Comte,' Christian murmured weakly in French.

'Of course.' François nodded as he answered in the same language. 'Do you remember being shot, *monsieur*?' The butler looked down at him quizzically.

Christian frowned in concentration, trying to recall— Dear Lord, yes, he remembered now. His groom's warning, followed by the sound of a shot being fired, the carriage coming to a halt and the door being thrown open, another two shots being fired, the arrival of the red-haired angel—

No, that last part was not right. It had not been an angel, but Lisette who had entered the carriage, before helping him outside so that they might both check on his groom, lying unconscious on the cobbled road.

'Pierre?' he prompted sharply.

François's eyes avoided meeting his. 'He is… not doing so well as you, *monsieur*, but Mademoiselle Lisette is doing all that she can for him.'

'Lisette…?'

'She is with Pierre now, Your Grace.' François

grimaced. 'Once she had attended to you, she turned her attention to Pierre and has remained with him all night. In fact, she has refused to leave his bedside.'

Christian could hear the admiration for Lisette in the older man's voice. Admiration fully deserved, if he was to understand the situation correctly; Lisette had not only doctored him last night but also Pierre. A task that would have sent most women of Christian's acquaintance running in the other direction. With the exception of his sister and the wives of his closest friends, of course. But every other woman Christian knew in society would have shrunk away from being asked to perform such a gory task.

A task he realised he was responsible for asking of her, as he recalled that he had refused to allow a doctor to be called for to attend either him or Pierre.

He had his reasons for that, of course. But Lisette was not privy to those reasons and had simply acted as he requested without explanation.

There was also the matter of her revelation that she was Helene Rousseau's daughter and not her niece to consider. Lisette's earlier claim, of having lived on a farm with relatives until just weeks ago, would explain why no one had known of the existence of Helene Rousseau's daughter before now.

A daughter Aubrey Maystone would have much interest in learning about.

'Take me to her.' Christian attempted to sit up.

'You will remain exactly where you are, Christian, and not undo all my good work of last night, unless you wish to feel the sharp lash of my tongue,' an imperious voice informed him firmly as Lisette stepped into the bedchamber.

Her own appearance was as dishevelled, if not more so than François's: her hair had escaped its pins and was falling down about her shoulders in untidy wisps; there were smears of blood on her cheek and throat, her black gown showing several darker stains which were almost certainly more blood. Her face was also deathly white, no doubt from spending a sleepless night attending to first Christian and then his groom, and her bottom lip was still slightly swollen from where Helene Rousseau had struck her.

And this was the young woman Christian intended to take back to England with him with the intention of handing her over to Aubrey Maystone.

Shame washed over Christian at the betrayal of such an act in the face of Lisette's selflessness last night. Not only had she brought them all home by driving the carriage then tended to both men's wounds all night, but by doing so she must also have known that she would be further incurring her mother's wrath, not only for having done those things but also by remaining out all night.

'Pierre?' he questioned softly.

She nodded. 'He has a slight fever, but I do not believe he will become any worse.' She placed a bowl of water and fresh bandages down on the bedside table.

'God be thanked,' Christian muttered gratefully; he already had enough on his conscience without the death of this innocent French groom.

All of the household staff were aware of his true identity, of course, were all loyal to the French Crown and aware of the danger they placed themselves in by working with him. But that did not mean that Christian wished to be responsible for the death of one of them.

'You, on the other hand, will remain in bed for the remainder of the day.' Lisette spoke firmly again. 'And tomorrow too, unless you wish for me to send for the doctor you refused to have attend you last night?'

Christian did not remember the last time a woman had spoken to him in so imperious a tone as this; his *grandmère*, before her death, and his sister Julianna tried to do the same, but Christian had grown adept at avoiding confrontation by meeting those dictates with a charming disregard for their content.

The determined expression on Lisette's face told him that the events of the night had stripped away all social politeness, and that she had no intention of being ignored nor charmed.

Besides, how could he possibly argue with the woman who was probably responsible for not only saving his own life but also that of the young French groom?

The young and handsome French groom,

Christian recalled with a displeased frown, with whom Lisette had sat up most of the night.

Which was utterly ridiculous of him in the circumstances.

His own clandestine presence in Paris was responsible for Pierre's injuries as well as his own, and also for Lisette's present exhaustion from doctoring them both. How could he possibly now feel jealous of the attention Lisette had necessarily shown the groom?

There was no logic or reason to it; it was just there, inside him. And, unlike the wound in his thigh, it felt as if it might be festering.

He smiled up at her. 'I have no intention of "going against doctor's orders" and getting out of bed, now that I can see for myself that you have come to no harm. I do, however, believe that you have done enough for both Pierre and myself for now and need to take your own rest.'

Lisette was well aware of how bedraggled she must look, after a night spent tending to Christian and his groom, and she certainly did not need him to remind her of it. 'It is my intention to break my fast before then returning to the Fleur de Lis to collect my things.'

'You are still intent on leaving there?'

'I cannot stay.' She shook her head. 'But first I will check your wound.' She indicated the bowl of water and fresh bandages.

'Is that necessary?'

'My— When I lived on the farm with the Du-prées, we found that if a wound was kept clean, with fresh bandages applied often, there was less chance of it becoming inflamed.'

'I am sure François will be only too happy to do that for me.'

'It is a little late for modesty now, *monsieur*.' Lisette eyed him impatiently as her attempts to pull back the bedclothes were met with resistance. 'I assure you, François and I have already seen all,' she now added drily.

In truth, she was no more comfortable with inspecting Christian's wound than he was in allowing her to do it now that he was fully conscious and aware of the intimacy. But she really had no choice in the matter. The wound must be looked at, and re-dressed if necessary.

The Comte's jaw tightened even as he slowly released the bedclothes. 'I believe you are enjoying my discomfort far too much, Lisette!'

Was she? Perhaps. It had been a long and eventful twenty-four hours, and she really had no patience, or strength, left to fight such a silly battle as this one.

Of the two, she was perhaps the most embarrassed as she and François carefully removed the bandage she had applied last night, Lisette's cheeks feeling hot with that embarrassment as she inadvertently touched the warmth of Christian's other inner thigh.

'I am sorry,' she muttered awkwardly as her hand instinctively pulled away, taking the bandage with it, which unfortunately was stuck to the wound at the front of his thigh. She winced as she saw a well of fresh blood instantly appear at the wound's surface.

It looked clean enough though, and there was no redness about it, so hopefully there would be no inflammation if she kept applying clean bandages; her foster mother had sworn by this method of avoiding inflammation to a cut or wound.

Tears filled her eyes as she now thought of the couple who had brought her up as if she were their own, and these horrible weeks since Helene Rousseau had brought her back to Paris with her.

No doubt this weakness of emotion was brought about by her tiredness and exhaustion, but that did not stop the emotion from being real. She missed the Duprées, and the quiet and simple life she had led with them, more than she could say.

'Lisette…?'

She brought herself back to her surroundings with a start—indeed, she was not sure how she could possibly have allowed her thoughts to stray in the first place, when she had a half-naked Christian Beaumont lying on the bed in front of her!

'I am very tired, *monsieur*.' She straightened. 'Perhaps, for your own safety, François should finish applying the rest of this clean bandage?' She looked questioningly at the butler, although he looked almost as tired as she did.

Christian frowned as he easily saw the signs of Lisette's exhaustion, in the paleness of her face and the slightly glazed look in her eyes. Her hands were also shaking slightly.

He turned to his butler. 'François, arrange for breakfast to be brought up to Mademoiselle Lisette in the blue bedchamber, followed by a hot bath, after which she is not to be disturbed for the rest of the day.' He had no doubt Lisette had already incited the wrath of her mother again by not returning to the tavern last night, so he couldn't see what further harm it could do if she did not return there for another day.

Her auburn brows rose. 'I see you are back to being your usual dictatorial self, *monsieur.*'

'Did I ever stop?' He eyed her ruefully.

She seemed to give the matter some thought before answering. 'No, I cannot say that you did.'

'And I see that you have developed a sharp tongue overnight,' Christian drawled.

'I am too tired to be any other way,' she admitted wryly.

'François will now take you to the blue bedchamber, arrange for breakfast and a bath to be brought up to you,' he decided briskly. 'And then both of you are to go away and get some sleep. The household can run without you for one day, François, a maid or footman can see to Pierre, and I am quite capable of wrapping a fresh bandage about my own leg—'

'Oh, but—'

'You will go with François now, Lisette,' Christian added firmly. 'Eat, bathe, rest.'

'If you undo all my good work—'

'Then I can expect to feel a further lashing of your tongue.' When he would much rather feel the soft caressing stroke of her hot, moist little tongue against any part of his anatomy.

Obviously, being shot in the thigh had not lessened his desire for this young woman in the slightest, Christian acknowledged self-derisively.

She nodded. 'That is exactly what you will feel, yes.'

Christian gave a throaty chuckle. 'Go, Lisette, and do not come back until you are completely rested and refreshed.'

Lisette really was too tired to argue any further as she followed François from Christian's bedchamber a short distance along the hallway to the 'blue bedchamber', a room so luxurious, with its white ornate furniture and blue carpets and blue satin drapes, both at the windows and about the huge four-poster bed, that she felt positively overwhelmed.

She turned to François. 'I do not need the use of such a lovely bedchamber as this—'

'The Comte believes you do. And so do I,' the butler added softly.

Lisette's cheeks warmed at the compliment. 'I do believe I might sleep for a week in such a comfortable-looking bed!' It certainly looked nicer than the slender cot she had been sleeping on at the tavern these past weeks.

François smiled. 'But first you must eat and bathe.'

Lisette looked at the dishevelled butler and then down at her own less than pristine appearance. 'We are a sorry-looking pair, are we not, François!'

He gave a boyish grin. 'We are merely battle-worn, Mademoiselle Lisette.'

Yes, 'battle-worn' correctly described how Lisette felt as she sank weakly down onto the stool in front of the dressing table once François had left to give instructions in regard to her breakfast.

She really had never seen such finery as the satins and velvets in this bedchamber, let alone thought she would ever sleep in such luxury.

But she had no doubt that, by leaving the tavern in the hurried way that she had last night, repugnant as returning to the Fleur de Lis was to her, if she did not go back to collect the few belongings she had, she now literally owned no more than the clothes she stood in—sat down in.

## Chapter Six

'I— But just yesterday, you said you had no plans to leave Paris as yet…'

Christian, having just told Lisette when she came to his bedchamber that evening that he had arranged passage for them both to go to England later tonight, could well understand her surprise.

He had kept his promise not to stir from his bed, but otherwise he had not been idle during the hours Lisette slept. Besides receiving continual updates on Pierre's condition—which seemed to be improving, thank God—and arranging passage to England for himself and Lisette, Christian had also sent out for several gowns and other female apparel for her.

She had protested, of course, but Christian had then pointed out that she could not continue to wear the soiled black gown. He was, after all, the reason she did not have anything but that soiled—and unattractive—black gown to wear.

The ordering of three new gowns had also allowed Christian to choose colours for her other than black. The deep purple gown she now wore and the pale and dark grey of the other two gowns were also mourning colours, but so much less sombre than that funereal black.

A mourning which he now knew to be for her uncle, the French spy André Rousseau.

Much as he might wish it, Christian knew he could not ignore or forget that fact.

His mouth firmed. 'You must know as well as I that the events of last night have necessitated changing my plans somewhat. As well as your own,' he continued softly. 'You already told me you intended leaving the tavern today anyway and it would perhaps be as well if you did not go back there at all. Unless there are things of your own there you cannot bear to be parted from?'

She grimaced. 'I have very few personal possessions...'

'Then leave them for now. There is no reason why you cannot claim them at a later date,' Christian added as she still hesitated.

She frowned. 'Even so, that does not mean I have any intention of travelling to England with you.'

Christian would much rather that Lisette came with him willingly; after all that she had done for him, he did not relish the idea of forcing her into accompanying him.

He wished he did not have to take her to England with him at all, knowing what fate awaited her there. But after last night he could not see a future for her here in Paris either. And if Lisette was as innocent as he believed her to be, then surely, once Aubrey Maystone had questioned her and realised her innocence for himself, Christian might be able to find a place for her in an English household, as a companion or governess, perhaps?

Perhaps his sister Julianna, expecting her first child in a few months' time, might even be persuaded into engaging Lisette as a nanny for the child?

*'Parlez-vous anglais?'* Christian asked her, to

which she gave a firm shake of her head. 'Then
shall have someone teach you the rudiments of
he language once we are in England.'

'Why?'

'You cannot live in another country and not
speak the language.' He eyed her frustratedly.

Whilst Lisette looked totally refreshed after
her rest, and the purple gown was most becoming to her creamy complexion and tidily upswept
red hair, Christian was feeling decidedly tired
and not a little bad-tempered after his busy day
making the necessary arrangements for their departure from Paris. It was now early in the evening and his thigh throbbed like the very devil
from his daytime exertions.

Lisette's eyes widened. 'Even if I were to agree
to accompany you now, I would not remain in
England longer than it takes to see you are safely
returned.'

'I doubt your mother will welcome you back
when, to all intents and purposes, you spent the
night here with me, before then travelling to
England with me,' Christian pointed out gently.

'She is not my mother! Biologically, perhaps,'

Lisette conceded reluctantly as Christian raised surprised brows. 'But I do not know her, had never even met her or knew of her existence until two months ago.'

'That is…hard to believe,' he murmured cautiously.

'Why is it?' Lisette stood up restlessly.

She now felt refreshed from her hours of sleep. Enough so that she had given thought to her present dilemma, and although she might accept that going to England with the Comte seemed the logical choice—the safest choice—for the moment, she could not think of remaining there. She was French, knew no other life than the one she had led with the Duprées, and briefly with Helene Rousseau here in Paris. One life was closed off to her, the other she had no wish to re-enter.

Even so, Lisette knew nothing of England or the English, apart from the fact they had been at war with France, under Napoleon's rule, for so many years.

She gave a shake of her head. 'I am sure I cannot be the first bastard child you have ever heard to have been fostered with strangers.'

'Unfortunately not,' he acknowledged tightly. 'But it is usual for that child to be aware they are being fostered. And who their real mother is.'

Was Lisette imagining the question in Christian's voice as he made that last comment? Did he doubt her claim of knowing nothing of Helene Rousseau's existence until just weeks ago?

'I assure you I did not,' she answered him tartly. 'Nor do I have any idea who my father is.'

'Madame Rousseau has not confided in you?'

'No.' Lisette stood in front of the window, the slowly flowing Seine glittering like silver in the moonlight. 'I am not sure I wish to know either, considering the…the type of man I know frequents the Fleur de Lis.' She repressed a shudder of distaste at the thought of one of the loutish and lowly men she had encountered there these past few weeks being her father.

Christian could totally sympathise with this sentiment after his visit to that establishment the evening before.

'Which brings me to another point, *mon—*

Christian,' she corrected at his frowning glance. 'Whatever you may have assumed to the contrary, I am nothing like Helene Rousseau. I have not, nor do I intend to take a lover or series of lovers.' Embarrassed colour glowed in her cheeks.

No doubt from thinking of the kisses the two of them had shared the night before. Far from innocent kisses, which could so easily have led to something deeper.

Christian's mouth twisted into a smile. 'I believe you will find I am somewhat…incapacitated, in any case, in that regard at present!'

'I am glad you find me so amusing, Christian.' She shot him an irritated glance for this show of levity. 'But your wounds will eventually heal.'

'You then expect I shall proposition you into agreeing to become my mistress?' Christian was finding this conversation less and less amusing by the minute.

Her cheeks flushed prettily. 'I can think of no other reason why you might take me to England with you.'

Christian wished that were the case! 'And if

were to make you a promise that I shall attempt not to do so?'

She blinked. 'Are you making me such a promise?'

Christian's jaw tightened. 'That I will promise not to attempt to do so, yes.'

She gave a typically Gallic sniff. 'Then I suppose that will have to do. But I still maintain that you cannot seriously expect to be able to travel back to England tonight. You will need to rest for several more days before even contemplating such a journey.'

'Whilst I have every confidence in François and my other employees here,' Christian bit out, 'I do not wish to put any of them in further danger by remaining in Paris longer than is necessary. I am well enough to travel to the ship later this evening,' he continued as she would have spoken. 'After which time I will retire to my cabin and, with your assistance, continue to rest for the remainder of the journey ho— to my estates in England.' He inwardly cursed himself for almost slipping up and calling England 'home'.

He knew he would have to reveal the truth of his identity before they docked in England. He had already sent on ahead for his ducal coach to be waiting for them at the quayside when they arrived. But, as he'd already decided, he would not do so until the ship was well under way and Lisette had no choice but to accompany him.

His appeal for her assistance on the journey, of playing upon the softness of her heart, was his way of ensuring she accompanied him.

Christian deplored even that subterfuge in regard to this young woman who had surely saved his life the previous night. And he fully intended to make his feelings on the subject known to Aubrey Maystone when he made his report to the older man; Lisette was not to come to any harm or Maystone would answer directly to him. But, powerful as the Duchy of Sutherland undoubtedly was, Christian knew that would still be no guarantee in regard to Lisette's future safety.

'I suppose that will have to do, if you are set on the idea…'

'I am,' Christian confirmed tautly. 'To that end, François has already arranged for my bags to be packed and the coach to be ready to leave for the docks in one hour's time.' And on this occasion Christian would ensure that the groom and driver accompanying them would be armed and ready to fight off anyone who tried to stop them from reaching the dockside.

Lisette realised, by the determined set of the Comte's jaw, that nothing she had to say would succeed in persuading him into altering those plans.

Having only just removed and hung up her new gowns and put away the pretty undergarments, Lisette now realised she would have to repack them all; grateful as she was for the new clothes, she still blushed to think of the intimacy of having Christian Beaumont order such things for her. No matter what he said to the contrary, it had the definite feel of a *patron* bestowing largesse upon his mistress.

Perhaps once she was in England, she would be able to find respectable employment for a time, and in that way repay him for the purchase of the new gowns and undergarments?

If so, Christian was right; she would need to

learn and speak English. 'Very well, *monsieur.*' This time Lisette ignored his frown of disapproval; if they were to travel to England together, then the formalities must be maintained in order to keep a distance between the two of them. A distance that had already been breached. Several times... 'I will return to my bedchamber and pack my own things now, and be ready to leave within the hour.'

Christian nodded his approval; he could not abide a woman who fussed and flounced and generally made a hullaballoo when it came to doing anything asked of her. Not that he had expected that of Lisette; she had already shown, time and time again, that she was made of much sterner stuff than to throw a tantrum because her plans had taken a sudden turn.

And he would protect her once they were in England, he vowed fiercely.

Against all and anyone who tried to harm her.

'I had no idea that sailing could be so invigorating as this!' Lisette smiled her happiness as she swept into Christian's cabin aboard the elegant sloop the following morning.

Any doubts that Christian might have had in regard to Lisette being a 'good sailor' had been dispelled the night before when, once on board the fast sloop, she had stayed up on deck conversing with the captain, who could speak and understand a rudimentary smattering of French—despite Christian's urgings for her to stay below deck—during the whole process of the ship setting sail and leaving the harbour.

This morning she looked even more bright-eyed and happily flushed in the cheeks.

Whereas Christian was in great discomfort from the wound to his thigh. Indeed, he had only managed to remove his boots the previous night before collapsing onto the bunk bed in which he now lay. He had then tossed and turned for most of the night, the swaying of the ship not helping in the slightest.

'At least one of us is pleased with the arrangement,' he snapped in disgruntlement.

Lisette's eyes widened at this show of bad temper from Christian; he had always seemed to be so calm and unruffled in their acquaintance to date. Even when he had been shot.

She studied his appearance more closely; his boots had been removed, but otherwise he seemed to have slept in his clothes—possibly because he had been unable to undress completely without assistance?

Assistance Lisette was ashamed to admit she had not thought to offer the previous night, in her enchantment with remaining on deck to watch as they set sail for England.

Christian's hair was also tousled and unkempt, there were dark shadows beneath those lavender-coloured eyes and his face had a greyish cast to it. Not a particularly good sign, but far better that he be pale in the face than flushed with a fever.

'I believe you will need to undress, so that I might look at your wound again,' she announced lightly—in an effort to hide the embarrassment she felt at the thought of the two of them being alone here when she helped Christian to remove his clothes.

She had not considered that, in her relief on discovering they had been given separate cabins aboard the ship, she would find herself completely alone with Christian when she came to his cabin; François had always been present when she had dressed Christian's wound whilst they were in Paris.

Christian scowled up at her. 'Do I look as if I am capable of undressing?'

Yes, the Comte was decidedly out of sorts this morning. 'I meant with my assistance, of course,' she came back pleasantly.

'Are you sure?' He quirked an impatient eyebrow. 'I would not wish to keep you from going up on deck and enjoying the rest of the voyage or to "damage your reputation"!'

Lisette ignored the jibe. Not only was it unworthy of the man she had come to know, but they must both be aware, even occupying separate cabins as they were, that her reputation would be 'damaged' forever, just from her having travelled alone with him to England.

Lisette had considered at the time, and still did, that it was a small price to pay in exchange for escaping, even only for a while, the life she had been forced to lead in Paris.

'I will help you to undress,' she repeated briskly. 'And then go and beg some hot water from the ship's cook to first help you wash and then to cleanse your wound. I will also need to acquire something I can use for clean dressings.'

'No doubt you are now on speaking terms with all the crew!' the Comte snapped accusingly as she crooked an arm beneath his to help him sit up higher against the pillows.

Yes, definitely out of sorts—and rude with it. 'The Captain was kind enough to introduce me to his officers and the men in the galley last night, yes,' Lisette answered distractedly, her expression deliberately neutral as she peeled the fitted jacket from him, before untying and removing his cravat and unfastening the buttons on his shirt.

Some of which she was sure Christian could have done for himself last night, but had perhaps been too tired or irritable to do so, after struggling to remove his boots. Men, her *maman* had once warned her, did not make good patients—mainly because they had no *patience* with their own weakness in having become sick in the first place. Although that could not be said of Christian's current predicament, when he had come by his present injury through no fault of his own.

Except in showing a marked interest in her.

Her own guilt over that was enough to cause Lisette to hold her tongue in regard to Christian's uncharacteristic bad temper as she lifted and then removed the shirt from his body.

Her breath caught in her throat when she turned back from depositing the soiled shirt on the floor and found herself looking at Christian's completely bared chest.

And what a chest it was—lightly tanned, with tautly defined muscles and just a light dusting of blond hair in the centre of his chest and tapering down to the waistband of his pantaloons.

Pantaloons Lisette now had to remove if she was to inspect and re-dress the wound on his thigh.

Christian inwardly acknowledged he was being less than gracious, let alone gentlemanly, this morning and, sensing Lisette's reluctance when it came to the unfastening of his pantaloons, he deftly released the buttons himself. But there was little he could do to help in regard to removing them; his leg now felt so stiff and sore he could barely move it.

Lisette's slightness of stature, and the height of the bunk bed upon which Christian lay, meant that her breasts were almost on a level with his chest, allowing soft wisps of her silky hair to brush across the bareness of his skin as she bent over the bed and struggled to peel back the pantaloons.

His manhood, in complete rebellion with how debilitated the rest of his body felt, instantly sprang to attention. Noticeably so, as Christian finally lay back weakly against the pillows wearing only his drawers.

That weakness was no doubt being increased because all the available blood seemed to have now gathered in his engorged member!

Had he ever suffered such an embarrassing moment as this before? Not that Christian could recall, no.

'I will go and collect some hot water from the galley.' Lisette was obviously aware of his physical response, her cheeks having flushed a becoming pink as she deliberately kept her gaze above the waistline of his drawers before she turned away and hurried from the cabin.

Christian stared up at the ceiling as he cursed the physical evidence of his arousal and wondered how he could possibly feel desire at a time like this. Admittedly, Lisette looked beautiful this morning, in her gown of pale grey and her face aglow with good health and humour, but that really was no excuse for such an ungentlemanly display of visible arousal. Not that he had any control over the matter, but still…

As a consequence, he was not in the least surprised to see Lisette was accompanied by a young man when she bustled back into his cabin several minutes later.

'Davy is Cook's galley assistant,' Lisette introduced in an offhand manner as she stood aside to put on an apron the cook had also given her, whilst Davy placed the bowl of water down upon the chest of drawers beside the bunk on which the Comte reclined, a sheet now covering his lower body.

She could not quite bring herself to look directly at Christian as she laid down the clean towels and the cloths she had brought with her to use as a dressing, her cheeks having warmed the moment she re-entered the cabin, at the memory of his physical arousal. She had been more than happy to accept Cook's offer of having his young assistant return to the cabin with her.

She was more grateful than ever for Davy's presence, having thrown back that covering sheet—and just as quickly replacing it again—after discovering that Christian had managed to remove his drawers in her absence and was now completely naked beneath that flimsy sheet.

Lisette pressed her lips together to stop herself from gasping out loud. Which in no way helped to eliminate the image now firmly imprinted in the forefront of her brain.

She had been too tired, whilst attending to Christian's wound through the night at his home in Paris, to be overly concerned by the dangerously predatory man himself.

A night of deep, restful sleep and the exhilaration of sailing to England, and Lisette found it far less easy to dismiss the raw masculine beauty of the man—flat and muscled abdomen, lean hips and long elegant legs, with dark blond curls surrounding his still semi-erect member.

The same man who just minutes ago had physically responded so visibly merely to her proximity.

As she now felt her own body responding to him…

Since meeting Christian, and being kissed by him, Lisette now recognised these signs of arousal in her own body for exactly what they were—the warmth in her cheeks, the tightness of her breasts, the tips sensitive and tingling, and the sudden damp heat between her thighs.

She sensed lavender-coloured eyes upon her as she arranged the sheet over Christian in such a way as to save them both further embarrassment, her movements deliberately brisk as she had Davy assist her in removing the soiled bandage. 'The Captain says we have made good time, the tide and winds having been kind to us, and so should be arriving in Portsmouth within the hour,' she remarked conversationally after folding back the bandage and looking at Christian's wound.

It looked raw and uncomfortable, but there did not appear to be any unusual sign of redness or pus, either back or front of that muscled thigh. No doubt Christian's discomfort was mainly caused by the exertions created by his having insisted they set sail last night, rather than remain in Paris to rest his leg and allowing the wound to heal, as she had advised he should.

Not that she was about to rebuke Christian for that again; he did not appear to be in the sort of mood today to tolerate any such chastisement, from her or anyone else.

Although she very much doubted he would be well enough to continue with their journey on to London by coach once they had reached Portsmouth; just the thought of his being jostled and bounced about inside a coach for hours was enough to make her wince.

'Cook has given me a salve to apply to your wound.' Lisette looked down dubiously into the stone jar before lifting it to her nose and sniffing at the contents. The mixture was a rather unattractive shade of pale brown, and she thought she could also detect the smell of lavender and cinnamon, no doubt in an attempt to override the strong smell of goose fat. 'Perhaps once I have cleansed the wound it would be as well not to tamper with the body's own healing qualities.' She quickly placed the stone jar back on the bedside cabinet before wiping her hands on her apron.

Christian's discomfort had eased since the bandage and soiled dressing had been removed, and he now held back a smile as he saw Lisette's obvious distaste for the cook's salve. 'Perhaps that would be as well,' he conceded drily.

Of course his tension might have been eased simply because he now knew he would be back on English soil within the next hour. In truth, the swaying and pitching of the sloop had almost certainly added to his suffering during the night. Just the thought of being able to depart this infernal swaying boat was enough to lift his spirits somewhat.

Enough so that he grinned at Lisette as she carefully used a pristine white cloth dipped in warm water to clean his wound; if he was not mistaken, it was one of the linen squares no doubt used in the dining room by the officers of the sloop. 'I really must commend your "bedside manner" as being as near perfection as I have ever known, Lisette,' he drawled just for the pleasure of seeing the blush that instantly warmed her cheeks at his deliberate double entendre.

A double entendre he doubted that Davy would understand, considering he and Lisette were talking in French and all the crew aboard the sloop were English. A fact Lisette had not yet remarked upon but which he was sure, with her quickness of mind, she must be well aware of and would no doubt question him on once they were safely on English soil.

'Perhaps you should reserve judgement, Monsieur le Comte, until after you have been attended by a physician and he is certain there is no need to have the leg amputated?' she retorted sweetly.

The little *chat* continued to flex her newly discovered claws, Christian acknowledged appreciatively as he settled back more comfortably against the pillows. 'It is unkind of you to punish me in that way, Lisette, even teasingly.'

She glanced up at him. 'If your wound does not become inflamed and full of pus, then it will not be because of anything you have done to prevent it!'

Ah, the lovely Lisette was still put out because he had chosen to ignore her words of caution the night before. 'It is not attractive in a woman to bear a grudge, Lisette,' he responded drily.

'And it is not attractive in a man to behave so *tête de cochon*,' she came back pertly.

Christian chuckled softly at hearing himself described as being 'pig-headed'. He preferred to think of himself as determined or strong-willed, but obviously Lisette saw it differently. 'I promise you that once we are back on English soil I will do everything within my power to facilitate my complete recovery.' He placed a hand over his heart as part of that pledge.

'Indeed.' Lisette eyed him mockingly as she finished cleansing his wound, believing in that moment that this man's arrogance alone was enough to prevent the wound from becoming inflamed.

He grinned at her unabashedly. 'I feel better already just knowing I will very soon be stepping off this constantly rocking boat onto terra firma!'

'I doubt you will be "stepping" anywhere with any degree of comfort or balance.' She began to apply the clean bandage. 'As I also doubt that you will be well enough for several more days to continue the journey on to London.'

Christian had already thought of that and, much as it irked him to admit it, he knew that a long journey by coach was not something he could contemplate right now. It would have to be enough, for the moment, that he was back in England. The delay would necessitate that he, and consequently Lisette, must tarry for a day or so in one of Portsmouth's more comfortable inns. An inn Christian had frequented many times before on his illicit travels to and from France, and of a kind only found away from the dockside. But there was no reason, whilst he languished there, that he could not send word to Aubrey Maystone, and the other Dangerous Dukes, of his safe return.

A frown creased his brow at the thought of Maystone's reaction to news of Lisette's presence in England. The last thing he wanted was for the other man to come to Portsmouth and take charge of the situation—of Lisette—whilst Christian was too incapacitated to stop him or defend her. No, perhaps he would wait awhile longer before apprising Maystone of the fact he was now back in England.

'Am I causing you discomfort?' Lisette prompted with concern as she saw the frown on Christian's brow.

'No more than usual,' he drawled as that frown lifted, lavender eyes now glittering with devilment.

The warmth in Lisette's cheeks seemed to have become a permanent fixture, and she glanced at Christian impatiently, knowing he meant to deliberately disarm her. That he was actually enjoying himself now at her expense.

Obviously, he was feeling slightly better, in temper as well as in physical comfort.

'Pity,' she snapped as she tightened and secured the bandage and saw him wince before she stepped away from the bunk bed. 'I will leave Davy to help you dress now, whilst I go to my own cabin and prepare for when we disembark.'

Christian's disappointed gaze followed her as she crossed the cabin before leaving; he was becoming too accustomed, he realised, to like and appreciate too much these scintillating conversations with Lisette.

'Ya ward's a pretty one, me lord.'

That scowl once again creased Christian's brow at Davy's shyly voiced praise for Lisette; indeed, if he was not careful, those lines between his eyes would be there to stay! Brought about, he had no doubt, by the advent of Lisette into his life.

And what was this nonsense of Lisette being his 'ward'?

An assumption by the crew, in view of their separate cabins? Or something that Lisette had told them in an effort to maintain some of the proprieties?

It made a certain sense, if he considered it. His

absence and incapacity below decks would have placed Lisette in a vulnerable position aboard the sloop inhabited only by men, and consequently she had perhaps considered it to be the wisest explanation for their travelling to England alone together. It was rather enterprising of her, in fact, and perhaps something Christian should have thought of himself.

Although he could not say he altogether cared for the way it placed him in the position of being a paternal figure to her in the eyes of others. Such as the fresh-faced Davy, now assisting him in dressing. A presentable and handsome young man who was of a similar age to Lisette.

Was Christian feeling the unfamiliar pangs of *jealousy* again?

He did not wish to answer that question.

But one thing he knew for certain—he did not appreciate Davy's obvious admiration for Lisette.

# Chapter Seven

'*The Duke of Sutherland?*'

Christian gave a wince at the accusation he could hear in Lisette's voice as she glared at him across the best bedchamber at The Dog and Rabbit Inn in Portsmouth.

He had intended to talk to her, tell her of his title, before they arrived at the inn. But in truth, he had been so discomfited by the time he departed the sloop, having also had to stand by as witness to Lisette bidding a fond farewell to the Captain before they could enter the waiting carriage, each jolt of that vehicle on the way here causing him immeasurable pain, that it had been all he could do to remain conscious.

Unfortunately, the landlord at the inn knew him only as the Duke of Sutherland and had greeted him as such, along with much bowing and scraping, as he accompanied the two of them up to the luxurious suite of rooms where Christian now gratefully reclined upon the bed in the main bedchamber.

He gave a dismissive shrug. 'It is merely another one of my titles.'

'The Duke of Sutherland is not "merely" another anything.' Lisette was now staring at him as if he were a creature come from another planet. 'Dukes are very important men in England, are they not? The elite of the aristocracy?'

Christian grimaced. 'I am not sure that "elite" quite—'

'Do not play games with me, Monsieur le Duc.' Lisette had hardly been able to believe her own ears when she heard the landlord of this fashionable inn address Christian so formally. A duke! She had felt completely out of her depth knowing he was the French aristocrat the Comte de Saint-Cloud, but this—an English duke—was beyond her comprehension.

Perhaps…

Lisette narrowed her eyes. 'You are not at all

what you pretend to be, are you…?' It had just occurred to her that an English duke would not have frequented a lowly Parisian tavern such as the Fleur de Lis.

'I do not pretend to be anything, Lisette,' Christian answered her firmly. 'I have every right to use the title of Comte de Saint-Cloud, as well as that of the Duke of Sutherland. I merely prefer, when I am in France and in such places as the Fleur de Lis, not to flaunt the English title.'

It made a certain sense, Lisette conceded reluctantly; the war between France and England might be over, but in some quarters of France it would still be painting a target upon any man's back for him to admit to being English. In a lowly French tavern such as the Fleur de Lis, it could have been lethal.

It might also be, she acknowledged grudgingly, that the Duke of Sutherland would not wish English *société* to know of his visit to such a bawdy establishment.

And yet…

Christian Beaumont—if that was even his true name—had never seemed to her the type of man who would come to the tavern in search of a willing woman to share his bed. Or possibly a man—since arriving at the tavern, Lisette had become aware of such relationships.

This man had drunk his share of wine that first evening, yes, and flirted a little with Brigitte and also with her, but it had not been an overt or predatory flirtation such as she had witnessed in the past of members of the aristocracy in search of a night's bawdy entertainment.

Her mouth thinned. 'You are English, then, rather than French?'

Another grimace. 'I am, yes.'

'Did Helene know this?' Lisette now eyed him speculatively. 'Is that the reason she pressed a pistol to your back that first evening?'

Christian would have much preferred to have had this conversation when he was not feeling at such a physical disadvantage. Although he acknowledged that might not be for some time, and Lisette was certainly entitled to some sort of explanation from him. An explanation he doubted she would take too kindly to.

'I believe the lady to have stated at the time

that her reason for doing so was as a warning for me to stay away from you,' he answered mildly.

Lisette's eyes widened before narrowing again. 'You did not answer my question, Monsieur le Duc. Did Helene know who you were that night?'

Christian could have continued to avoid answering the question directly, but he knew by the angry glitter in Lisette's eyes and the same flush of anger in her cheeks that it would not be wise for him to do so. Lisette might bear no physical resemblance to the woman who was her mother, but he now knew she most certainly shared the older woman's fiery temperament. He might just find himself at the receiving end of another pistol if he continued to fob Lisette off with half-truths and lies.

He sighed deeply. 'Following events would appear to indicate that as being the case, yes.'

'Following—? *Mon Dieu*, Helene's reason for sending her attackers against you had nothing to do with the attention you showed towards me,' Lisette gasped in realisation, 'and everything to do with her knowing you are an English *spy*?'

Christian shifted uncomfortably. 'I do not believe I have admitted to being any such thing—'

'You do not need to do so,' Lisette interrupted in disgust as she began to pace the bedchamber restlessly. It all made so much sense to her now.

Helene's warnings that night regarding associating with the Comte de Saint-Cloud.

Helene's desire to have the Comte killed.

*The fact that Lisette had found Christian lurking in a doorway across from the tavern later that evening.*

He had not been waiting there for her, but spying on Helene and the people who entered the tavern after it had closed for the night.

Just as Helene had not been concerned for her welfare but instead attempting to keep her away from a man she knew to be spying on her and her associates.

It also explained the attempt of Helene's cutthroats to kill *le Duc* in the middle of the street.

*And their flight to England the following night.*

It all made such sense to Lisette now.

Perfect—and humiliating—sense. She had thought—believed—that he had enjoyed and been as aroused by their kisses as she had, and all the time—

Christian winced as he had difficulty keeping up with—translating—the tirade in French that now followed his admission, Lisette's accusations and insults flowing forth without pause from that highly kissable mouth. Obviously, not all of Lisette's time at the French tavern had been wasted.

*English bastard* he understood. Followed by such a barrage of other insults and names he had no chance of deciphering one from the other.

Instead, he decided to lie back against the pillows and allow Lisette to give vent to her anger. He might not be able to keep up with those insults, but he did know he deserved everything she might accuse him of being.

Lisette's shock and outrage were also further proof, if he should need it, that she really was everything she appeared to be—a young innocent caught in the middle of a dangerous game she did not know of or comprehend.

Now all Christian had to do was convince Maystone of the same.

All?

Following the abduction and kidnapping of his grandson, even if he was eventually safely returned, Aubrey Maystone was not currently in a forgiving or tolerant mood. It would take more than Christian's opinion on the matter to persuade that gentleman into accepting Lisette's innocence. Especially if the other man should realise Christian's opinion was not impartial where Lisette was concerned.

As he had demonstrated only too clearly these past few days, a man could not hope to hide his physical response to a woman. And Aubrey Maystone was nothing if not astute.

Which meant that Christian—

'Are you even listening to me?' Lisette challenged, becoming even more outraged as she noted his distraction. 'Of course you are not. Why should a *duc* care for the opinion of a woman he knows to be Helene Rousseau's daughter, and no doubt considers to be nothing more than a French *putain*—?'

'You go too far, Lisette!' Christian's voice was a low and dangerous growl, a warning that all who knew him would most certainly have taken heed of.

But not Lisette. 'I will go as far as I wish, *Your Grace*—' she somehow managed to make the formal title sound every bit as insulting as the word *putain* '—when you obviously misled me from the very first words you ever spoke to me!'

As those 'very first words' had been his false surname and title, Christian could not deny the accusation. 'I am Christian Algernon Augustus Seaton, Fifteenth Duke of Sutherland, as well as numerous other titles, at your service, *mademoiselle*. I trust you will forgive me if I do not get up and present a formal bow?' he added with self-derision for his recumbent and incapacitated figure on the bed.

Lisette's present feelings of humiliation were such that she could forgive this—this *duc* nothing. Helene's treatment of her had been hard enough to bear, but to realise, to now know, that Christian *Seaton* had only been using her to get close to Helene, and in the process play Lisette for the fool, was beyond forgiveness.

She straightened, her spine rigid with the anger

she felt. 'No, I do not forgive you, Your Grace. Nor do I intend remaining in your company, or your vicinity, a moment longer—'

'You cannot leave, Lisette—'

'I do not believe you are in any condition to prevent me from doing exactly as I wish!' She eyed him scornfully as he sank back weakly against the pillows after having sat up abruptly, obviously with the intention of standing up, until the pain of the movement became too much for him. 'I am not completely heartless, and will arrange for a doctor to be sent to attend you before I leave, but—'

'The landlord here believes you to be my ward—'

'—be assured, I do not intend— Why would you claim such a thing, now that we are back in England?' Lisette frowned across at him.

Irritation creased Christian Seaton's brow. 'I felt compelled, as you did aboard the sloop,' he added pointedly, 'to give some explanation for our travelling together without benefit of a valet or maid.' He grimaced. 'I felt it best for all con-

cerned, now that we have arrived in England
to continue with that pretence.'

'I do not believe you *felt* anything or gave the
matter a moment's consideration, where I am
concerned, Monsieur le Duc.' Lisette glared her
anger at him. 'You had no thought other than
your own need to avert a scandal.' She turned
on her heel and marched to the door of the bedchamber. 'I only agreed to accompany you to
England because of concern for your injury, but
now that you are arrived safely I have no intention of remaining here with you a moment longer—'

'I cannot allow you to leave, Lisette.'

'You cannot *allow*?' She spun back to face
him, her cheeks warm with temper and the need
to hold back the tears now stinging her eyes; she
would not cry in front of this man.

Since the Duprées had died so suddenly, Lisette had been plunged into a life such as she had
never imagined possible. That she now found
herself in England, an outcast from her own people and country, and completely at the mercy of

the false-faced Christian Seaton's whims and fancies, was beyond enduring.

'I shall go when and where I please, *monsieur*,' she informed him stiffly. 'And neither you nor anyone else shall stop me.'

'You are a woman alone, without funds, and as such you are vulnerable—'

'I am more aware of what that means than you are, I assure you,' Lisette said scornfully. 'But I would rather sell my soul to the devil than be beholden to you for a moment longer!'

A nerve pulsed beside Christian's thinned lips, his jaw clenched as he attempted to maintain a hold on his own temper. 'Believe me, alone in a foreign land and without money, it is not your soul you would have to sell in order to survive.'

Her face paled, even those pouting lips having become a pale rose colour, her eyes dark and haunted. 'I despise you utterly.'

If she had said those words with venom, with any trace of emotion at all, Christian might have known what to say in return. As it was, he could only feel the cut of that emotionless statement from the top of his head to the toe of his boots.

'I do not feel the same way about you, Lisette,' he told her huskily. 'Far from it, in fact,' he added drily for the evidence she had seen just that morning regarding his body's reaction to her.

She eyed him scathingly. 'Then that is your misfortune, *monsieur*, because I most assuredly now despise you.'

Christian could see that emotion burning fiercely in her eyes. And she was only going to hate him more once she met Maystone and knew of Christian's real motivation in bringing her to England with him. 'But you will stay anyway.' It was a statement, not a question.

Lisette drew in a ragged breath. 'And what happens when your "ward" suddenly disappears? When I have returned to France? What lies will you tell about me then?'

The truth was Christian had no idea what the future held for Lisette.

He only knew his own need to protect her as much as he could. And publicly claiming her as his ward now he was back in England was the only way he knew to do that.

'As you are now acknowledged as being my ward, I will be perfectly within my rights to hunt you down and bring you back if you should attempt to run away from me,' he stated evenly.

'You—'

'Just as, as your guardian, I would also be perfectly within my rights to hunt down anyone who attempted to hurt you,' he added softly, understanding now why his close friend Griffin Stone, the Duke of Rotherham, had once felt pressed to claim his now wife as his ward. As he had also discovered, for a single gentleman it was the only way in which to protect an unprotected female who had no one else to care what happened to her.

And Christian did care what happened to Lisette. Very much so.

'—are an arrogant—' Lisette stared at him suspiciously. 'Why should anyone attempt to hurt me? I do not know anyone in England. Or they me.' She looked puzzled.

The time for truth, Christian acknowledged with an inner wince. 'Unfortunately, that is not true of your mother—'

'Helene?' Lisette looked even more mystified. 'As far as I am aware, she does not know anyone here either—' She broke off to look at him searchingly. 'This has something to do with the fact that you were in Paris spying upon her, doesn't it?'

'Did you know your uncle, André Rousseau?'

Lisette stilled. 'I believe I told you that he died before I arrived in Paris…'

'I believe you did too.'

'And?'

Christian Seaton grimaced. 'And I have no way of confirming whether that is the truth.'

Lisette's chin tilted challengingly. 'Unlike you, Your Grace, I do not lie.'

His mouth thinned at the rebuke. 'I did not start out with the intention of lying to you, Lisette.'

'That may be true,' she allowed grudgingly. 'But you are certainly responsible for continuing to do so.'

He grimaced. 'I had no way of knowing if you were to be trusted with the truth.'

Lisette gave what she knew to be a humourless smile. 'You still do not.'

'True,' the Duke conceded. 'But we are on English soil now.'

They were, yes, and, despite Lisette's outward show of bravado, she was more than a little unnerved by being in a strange country where she knew no one. Except the man who had been lying to her from the moment they first met. A man whose reason for being in Paris had been to spy on Helene Rousseau.

'What did you hope to learn by watching Helene?' she prompted cautiously; she knew that the woman who was her mother had been plotting and planning—even if Lisette had no idea of the details of those plots and plans—during those late night and secret meetings in a room above the tavern. But she had no way of knowing how much Christian Seaton knew of those meetings, or indeed Helene herself.

In the circumstances, sadly perhaps more than Lisette knew herself, in regard to the latter.

'How much do you know of her…nocturnal activities?'

Lisette blinked. 'I am uncertain of your meaning,' she came back cautiously.

Christian could not help but smile ruefully at Lisette's guarded response to his question. No, there might not be any physical similarities between Lisette and her mother, but the intelligence was most certainly there.

'Oh, I believe you understand me perfectly.' He nodded. 'That you are well aware your mother is a Parisian who has no affection for her own King.' He paused but Lisette offered no reply. 'Your uncle, André Rousseau, was another. He came to England two years ago under an assumed name, to work as tutor to the son and heir of an English earl. During the year he spent here he set up a network of spies, within the homes of many members of society as well as the English government,' he continued evenly. 'Their ultimate intention was to assassinate the Prince Regent, as well as the other leaders in the coalition, and thus cause chaos within those countries which would allow the newly escaped Bonaparte to march on Paris and resume his place as Emperor of France.'

Lisette was so shocked by what Christian was telling her that her legs felt so weak she now stumbled her way across the bedchamber to drop down onto the chair beside the window before answering him. 'That is incredible.'

'But nevertheless true.'

She swallowed with difficulty, her mouth having suddenly become very dry.

'To achieve their goal they kidnapped the young grandson of a powerful man behind the English government, threatening to kill the boy if that gentleman did not hand over certain information regarding the date and locality of Bonaparte's second incarceration,' the Duke continued remorselessly.

'No…!' Lisette felt her face pale.

'Yes,' he confirmed grimly. 'Luckily, we were able to rescue the boy in time, without that necessity, and so prevent Bonaparte from escaping a second time.'

'And you believe—you are of the opinion Helene was involved in this plot?' Lisette felt sick at the thought.

Although why she should be she had no idea;

Helene had already demonstrated, by not so much as bothering to see or visit her own child once during the first nineteen years of that child's life, that she was not in the least maternal. Nor, apparently, was she afflicted with any softer feelings in regard to a child's life.

'Your uncle, André Rousseau, was instrumental in setting these plans in motion, but I believe that it was your mother, Helene Rousseau, who was responsible for seeing that those plans were carried out after his death.' He nodded tersely.

Lisette moistened the dryness of her lips before speaking. 'I had no idea...'

Christian so much wanted to believe that. He *did* believe that. Convincing Maystone of the same was the stumbling block.

His discomfort now owed nothing to his wounded thigh and everything to do with what he had to say next. 'There are...people in England who will wish to speak with you, Lisette.'

'Me?' She looked shocked at the idea.

He grimaced. 'You are as close to Helene Rousseau as we are likely to get—'

'I am not close to her at all!' Lisette protested. 'I hardly know her.'

'Nevertheless, you are her daughter.'

Lisette took in the full import of Christian's words. 'You are hoping to use me in some way in order to influence Helene's future actions.'

A nerve pulsed in Christian's clenched jaw. '*I* am hoping to protect you; others may wish to do otherwise.'

Lisette no longer knew what to think.

That Helene could be involved in something so monstrous as kidnapping a child was abhorrent to her.

That *she* would be used as a similar weapon against Helene was also obvious.

She gave a shake of her head. 'Helene will not be swayed by any threats that are made towards me.'

Unfortunately, Christian also believed that to be the truth; fanatics such as Helene and her brother André were not people who allowed personal emotions to enter into their bigger plans. Something else he would need to convince Maystone of.

In the meantime, as he had suspected, he had now succeeded in frightening Lisette with the truth. 'I will not allow anyone to hurt you—'

'And how will you stop them?' Lisette rose abruptly to her feet as she looked at him coldly. 'I should have known that your interest was never in me, that I was merely a convenient pawn for you to use in the continued war against Napoleon!'

'That is not true—'

'It is true, and you know that it is!' Tears glistened in those beautiful blue eyes. 'I cannot believe, after I helped to save you from your attackers, and then nursed you through the night and on the voyage to England, that you were all the time being so deceitful!' She turned on her heel and ran to the door.

'Lisette—!' Christian once again attempted to sit up and swing his legs to the side of the bed with the intention of rising to his feet, ignoring the pain as he pushed up unsteadily onto his feet, wanting only to reach Lisette, to prevent her from leaving, to reassure her—

'Well, well, well, and what have we here?' drawled an all too familiar voice.

Christian felt himself toppling and then falling back onto the bed as he looked up and saw his brother-in-law Marcus Wilding, the Duke of Worthing, standing in the doorway with Lisette an unwilling prisoner in his arms.

## Chapter Eight

'Can you manage, Christian, or shall I release this beauty in order to assist you?'

Christian glared across the bedchamber at his brother-in-law as he carefully sat up on the bed; Marcus was one of his best friends as well as his brother-in-law, but that did not change the fact that he also had an infuriating knack for the understatement.

'Ah, I see you have decided to manage on your own.' Marcus's green eyes were alight with curiosity. 'Perhaps you would care to make the introductions?' He arched a pointed black brow at the young woman whose wrist he now held securely in order to prevent her from leaving.

Christian's glare turned to a scowl. 'What are you doing here, Marcus?'

The other man looked completely unruffled, by Christian's taciturn tone and Lisette's continued efforts to release herself.

'I am here to see you, of— Ouch!' Marcus looked down in surprise as one of Lisette's tiny booted feet came down painfully on his instep. 'A hellion, by God!' he murmured admiringly.

Christian *would* have warned the other man, in regard to Lisette's temper, if he was not feeling quite so out of sorts with Marcus himself.

Having sent word ahead for his coach to arrive in Portsmouth, he should perhaps have realised that his overprotective sister, and consequently his totally besotted brother-in-law, would keep themselves apprised of his movements.

'Just so,' he confirmed drily as he settled himself more comfortably on the side of the bed. 'Lisette, the man you just assaulted is Marcus Wilding, the Duke of Worthing, and married to my sister Julianna.'

Lisette ceased her struggles instantly to instead look up at the devilishly handsome man holding her prisoner; green eyes were dancing merrily down at her as he met what was no doubt her shocked gaze.

Of course she was surprised at meeting yet another duke; indeed, she seemed to be meeting more than her fair share of them recently.

'And you are…?' this new duke queried pointedly.

'I am—'

'Lisette Duprée, my ward,' Christian Seaton answered the other man challengingly, or so it seemed to Lisette.

And no doubt it was; if this was Christian Seaton's brother-in-law, then he must know that the other man did not have a ward. Or, at the very least, he had not done so the last time the two of them had met.

'My ward,' Christian repeated firmly.

'Your *French* ward?' The Duke of Worthing arched questioning brows.

'As I said.' The other man nodded stiffly.

Lisette now found herself the focus of Marcus Wilding's narrowed gaze as he obviously tried to make sense of Christian's announcement. 'I am—I was—I am travelling to visit my relatives in England, *monsieur*, and His Grace was kind enough to offer to act as my guardian for the duration of the voyage.' A guilty blush coloured her cheeks even as she spoke the lie.

'Really?' Those dark brows arched even higher. 'She speaks no English at all, Christian?' He addressed the other man in that language.

Christian's jaw tightened at the almost accusatory tone he could hear in his brother-in-law's voice. 'I will explain all later, Marcus.'

'I am not the one you will need to explain yourself to,' the other man assured him ruefully.

'Maystone—'

'I was thinking more of Julianna, actually,' Marcus drawled mockingly. 'Although I am sure Maystone will be interested in this...development too.'

Christian frowned at thoughts of both Julianna and Maystone. But the die had been cast now, his claim made, and he had no intention of abandoning Lisette to interrogation by either Maystone or Julianna.

'Care to explain the reason why you're currently…incapacitated?' His brother-in-law indicated his injured thigh.

'Again, not now,' Christian answered tightly.

Amusement darkened Marcus's eyes. 'The hellion did not shoot you, did she?'

Christian's eyes narrowed. 'No.'

'Then perhaps one of her outraged relatives?'

That question was far too close to the truth for Christian's liking. 'Stop enjoying yourself at my expense, Marcus, and tell me—is Julianna well?' He was fully aware this was the easiest way in which to divert Marcus; the other man enjoyed nothing more than talking of the wife he adored.

'Very.' Marcus instantly beamed.

'My sister is *enceinte*, Lisette.' Christian included her in the conversation as she looked at them both curiously.

'*Mon félicitations, monsieur,*' she offered warmly.

'*Merci, madamoiselle.* You really must do something about this only speaking French, Christian.' Marcus frowned. 'It will not go down well in some quarters.'

'I intend to do so.' In truth, it seemed that Lisette had already acquired a smattering of English; several of the names she had called him earlier—in heavily accented English—were worthy of a dockside sailor. Which, no doubt, was exactly from whom she had heard them!

'The two of you seemed to be having…some sort of disagreement when I arrived?' Marcus glanced at him questioningly.

'A difference of opinion, that is all,' Christian dismissed.

Marcus's brows rose. 'Sounded a bit more than that to me, old chap.'

'Well, no doubt as a married man you would know more about such differences of opinion than I!' Christian came back tersely.

'Not so, Christian. Julianna and I rarely, if ever, differ in opinion,' the other man dismissed loftily.

'That is because Julianna thinks you are a conceited ass and you know that you are!'

'Something like that.' Marcus grinned unabashedly before sobering. 'You realise Maystone will have to be informed of both your return and your injury.'

'But not immediately.' He would much prefer it if he was not at a disadvantage, caused by his wound, when he spoke with the older man.

Marcus shrugged. 'Not sure how that's going to be possible, Christian. We were not the only ones awaiting word of your return, and the moment he learned you had sent for your carriage, Maystone dispatched me here to meet you and accompany you back to London. He wishes you to report to him immediately as to your findings.'

Christian deeply regretted having sent for his carriage at all, if that was the case. 'That is obviously not possible in my present condition.' He grimaced.

'Obviously.' His friend nodded. 'What do you want me to tell Maystone when I return to London later today?'

Christian felt no surprise at hearing Marcus intended to return to the capital today, with or without him. Previously a profligate rake, Marcus was now totally devoted to Julianna and the baby they were expecting; no doubt he could not bear the thought of being separated from her, even for a single night. It pleased Christian that his sister and his friend had found such happiness together.

At the same time it in no way helped him to find a solution to this present dilemma. 'You could always tell Maystone I have not arrived as yet?'

The other man grimaced. 'In which case, he will have expected me to linger in Portsmouth until you do.'

Damnation.

'Perhaps, Your Grace,' Lisette was the one to put in softly, 'you might tell this gentleman, of whom you both speak so respectfully, the truth? That Christian was injured whilst involved in the work for which the gentleman named Maystone no doubt sent him to Paris?'

Both men turned to look at her in astonishment. Rightly so; it might have been rude of them to do so, but their conversation had all taken place in English.

Lisette steadily returned their shocked gazes.

'I said I did not speak English, Your Grace, not that I did not understand it.'

*Hell* and damnation!

Christian had been under the misapprehension all this time that Lisette did not understand any conversation spoken in English. To now learn that she had knowledge of the language made him question any and all of those conversations unguardedly spoken in front of her.

Could it be that she *was* indeed a spy for her mother, Helene Rousseau?

Until a few moments ago Christian would have staked his life on that not being the case. The revelation that Lisette understood English, even if she did not speak it, meant he was now less certain. A *lot* less certain. Especially as he and Marcus had not exactly been discreet in their own conversation.

Christian felt sick at the very thought of travelling to London today. But did he really have a choice? Marcus would return to London today regardless, and with Christian unable to move from his bed, Lisette would then be free to roam Portsmouth. With the idea of making contact with one of her mother's cohorts? Christian knew that he could no longer trust his own judgement in regard to Lisette.

He breathed deeply in resignation. 'If you will allow me to rest for a few hours, Marcus, Lisette and I will accompany you back to London later today—'

'I am not going to London—'

'I think that might be for the best, Christian.'

Lisette and the Duke of Worthing spoke at the same time, the one to protest the idea, the other to agree to it.

Lisette gave the Duke of Worthing a disapproving frown before stepping back into the bedchamber to glare at Christian Seaton. 'I do not wish to go to London, and you cannot travel anywhere in your present condition!'

He gave a weary shrug. 'I believe I must.'

'You will undo all of my efforts to prevent your wound from becoming inflamed if you attempt to do so,' Lisette maintained stubbornly as she came to stand beside the bed.

Christian looked up at her ruefully. 'I would have thought such discomfort might please you, considering the names you called me a short time ago?'

Lisette blushed at the memory of some of the names she had called him in temper. Not wholly undeserved, but still…

She raised her chin. 'You have deceived me,' she stated. 'Nor does your duplicity have anything to do with this present conversation.'

'No?'

'No!' she snapped impatiently. 'I have spent the past twenty-four hours ensuring that you have every opportunity to recover from your wound.'

'And, if I am not mistaken, just minutes ago you consigned me to the devil—'

'Much as I am enjoying this exchange,' Marcus Wilding cut in drily, 'I do not see that it is achieving much.'

'Oh, do be quiet, Marcus!'

Lisette continued to glare at the Duke of Worthing. 'Christian—His Grace, received a bullet wound to his thigh only two nights ago. The voyage to England was madness, this—

travelling to London today—would be even more so.'

Christian felt Marcus's gaze on him as Lisette spoke. 'You really were shot...?'

He grimaced. 'A trifle—'

'The bullet passed straight through the flesh of your thigh,' Lisette contradicted impatiently.

'Julianna is going to be most displeased.' Marcus gave a wince. 'I assured her you would be in no danger during your visit to France.'

'That was rather reckless of you, Marcus,' Christian Seaton drawled.

The other man shrugged. 'I did not want her to worry in her condition.'

'Even so...'

'When you two gentlemen have quite finished!' Lisette frowned her frustration at them both. 'Thank you,' she bit out when she once again had the attention of both gentlemen. 'You are not going anywhere today,' she informed Christian. 'And neither are you,' she instructed the other man. 'If Christian must go to London, then it will have to be tomorrow, after he has rested today and had a night's sleep, and *you* will have to accompany him. I am sure, for the sake of her brother's health, that your duchess will not mind your absence for one night.'

'Oh, I don't know about that—'

'I should give it up, if I were you, Marcus,' Christian advised as he saw the implacability of Lisette's expression. 'When Mademoiselle Lisette takes on that particular mutinous expression, I have found it is in everyone's interest not to argue with her!'

Marcus's eyebrows shot up into his hairline.

Not surprisingly; Marcus was well aware that Christian's outwardly charming disposition hid a will of steel. It must be something of a surprise to the other man to learn that Christian appeared to have more than met his match in 'Mademoiselle Lisette'.

It had come as something of a surprise to Christian, after his assumption that first evening that she was a shy innocent.

'And while I am "resting and sleeping", what will you be doing…?' He now eyed Lisette guardedly.

'I will be out seeking employment and somewhere to stay whilst I earn the money to pay for my passage back to France,' she informed him pertly.

'Absolutely not.' Christian spoke firmly.

Those blue eyes sparkled with rebellion. 'You are a…' She trailed off, obviously not finding a word that adequately expressed her frustration. 'You do not have the right to tell me what I may or may not do— You find something amusing, Your Grace?' Lisette looked challengingly at Marcus Wilding as he began to chuckle.

This added challenge only seemed to increase the other man's humour rather than quell it, Marcus now consumed with laughter as he placed an arm about his waist before bending over slightly.

Christian allowed his friend his few moments of amusement at his expense, only too well aware of the reason for it; Christian Seaton, the Duke of Sutherland, was a man that few dared cross let alone berate and rebuke. Lisette had just done both.

'Oh, good Lord!' Marcus was wiping tears of laughter from his cheeks when he finally straightened. 'Never thought I would see the day!' He continued to chuckle. 'Wait until the other Dangerous Dukes hear about this.'

'Dangerous Dukes?' Lisette echoed guardedly.

'I will explain another time.' Christian dismissed her question with a pointed frown at Marcus; the six friends, the Dangerous Dukes, had earned that title because of their exploits in the bedchamber as much as their work for the Crown. Lisette already had enough of a bad opinion of him at the moment, without adding to it. 'I suggest, whilst I rest, that Marcus accompanies you down to luncheon. You have to eat, Lisette,' he added cajolingly as she looked set to refuse the suggestion.

It had been several hours since Lisette enjoyed a breakfast of fruit and bread aboard the sloop. Besides, she had no money as yet to be able to buy her own lunch. There was a time for pride and a time for practicality, and her empty stomach decided that luncheon fell into the latter category. 'If Monsieur le Duc is agreeable.' She gave the other man a polite smile.

'As if butter would not melt in her mouth,' Marcus noted admiringly.

*'Monsieur?'* Lisette looked at him in innocent enquiry.

'Never mind.' The Duke of Worthing ruefully shook his head before turning to Christian, who gave a pained groan as he attempted to once again lie down upon the bed. 'Do you think you will be well enough to travel to London tomorrow?' He frowned his concern. 'Perhaps we should call a doctor—'

'Le Duc has refused to have a doctor attend him.' Lisette shrugged her shoulders.

Christian completed his struggle to lie prone on the bed before answering her. 'Why call for a doctor when I have you to care for me, my dear Lisette?' He gave her a sweetly insincere smile.

Lisette was still angry with him, had no wish to find this man in the least amusing, nor did she wish to smile at his sarcasm, and yet she did not seem able to stop herself. 'I will not be here to attend to you after tomorrow,' she conceded exasperatedly; one more night, spent in the comfort of this inn, would not make too much difference to her ultimate plan to leave the company of Christian Seaton. 'Come, Monsieur le Duc, let us go and eat luncheon together.' She rested her gloved hand in the crook of Marcus Wilding's arm.

Christian scowled as Marcus shot him a mocking glance over his shoulder as he and Lisette departed the bedchamber together in search of the dining room downstairs.

Not that he was in the least troubled by thoughts of Marcus charming Lisette—as the other man had charmed so many other ladies before his marriage to Julianna. No, Christian had no such fears where his friend was concerned, knew of his complete devotion to Julianna; it was the fact that he was giving the matter any thought at all that he found so disturbing.

As he found the idea of Lisette remaining in Portsmouth disturbing.

And equally impossible.

Somehow, in some way, he knew he had to persuade Lisette into accepting that she had no choice but to accompany the two men to London.

When he would have to pass her over to the tender mercies of Aubrey Maystone's interrogation?

Not if he had anything to say about it!

And he would…

'Perhaps if you were to sit here beside me it would help to prevent my being jostled about so much…?' Christian looked persuasively across the carriage at Lisette.

She made no reply as she coldly returned that look; the two of them had not so much as spoken a word to each other since Christian's carriage departed Portsmouth earlier that morning.

Christian had tried the previous evening, in every way he could, to persuade Lisette that going to London with them, talking to Maystone herself, convincing that gentleman of her innocence, was by far the best course of action.

Marcus, apparently tired of the arguments, had decided to take the matter into his own hands this morning—no doubt feeling disgruntled after a night spent away from Julianna and their bed—and simply picked Lisette up in his arms and deposited her in Christian's coach, before instructing the groom to drive on.

Not an auspicious beginning to their journey!

Not that Marcus was the one who had to bear the brunt of Lisette's stony silence, that gentleman having chosen to ride ahead on his horse.

Lisette had not been silent either initially, of course, as she had once again reviled Christian with a list of insults that would have made a fishwife blush. After which she had fallen into this icy silence that was, quite frankly, causing Christian far more discomfort than his thigh.

Indeed, his thigh felt a little easier today, after the long rest yesterday and a night's sleep, and he had even managed to dress himself this morning, with Marcus's help, and eat a little of the breakfast brought up to his bedchamber.

Food that seemed to have settled uncomfortably in his stomach as the icy silence continued between himself and Lisette. 'I am not the one who picked you up and placed you—'

'Only because you are not yet well enough!' Her eyes flashed with anger. 'If you had been, I have no doubt you would have manhandled me as uncivilly as did Le Duc de Worthing.'

Christian gave a wince. 'Please come and sit beside me, Lisette.'

'Why?'

Because Christian badly needed to hold her in his arms. In truth, he had thought of doing little else since she had retired early to her own bedchamber the previous evening. No doubt with the intention of plotting and planning a way in which she might leave the inn and so avoid being made to accompany him and Marcus to London today.

When he had voiced that concern to Marcus, the other man had assured him that he had placed one of the inn's servants outside the door of Lisette's bedchamber to prevent such an occurrence.

'Please, Lisette.' Christian now patted the upholstered seat beside him. 'Or I shall be forced to come to you,' he added softly; after all, there was only so much space for Lisette to retreat inside his ducal carriage.

'You will do no such thing!' Lisette frowned at him. 'I may not like you or your friend very much at the moment, but neither do I wish you any further harm,' she acknowledged begrudgingly, having spent many wakeful hours of the night considering her position.

There was no doubting that Helene was indeed up to something nefarious during those late night clandestine meetings with her cohorts. Nor could Lisette change the fact that she was the other woman's daughter.

Consequently Christian could not know with any certainty that Lisette was not in cahoots with the older woman and had only accompanied him to England in order to gain information to further her mother's plot to undermine the English government and monarchy.

Which was not to say that Lisette in any way forgave Christian for deceiving her, only that she now understood it, in part.

Unfortunately for Christian, it was not the part of her that had been so attracted to this *Duc Dangereuse*.

Oh, yes, Lisette understood that sobriquet too now, having charmed Marcus Wilding into confiding in her when they dined together the previous evening.

Nor was she as self-confident and self-conained as she wished to appear in front of Christian. She felt completely vulnerable in this strange country amongst people she did not know. She also feared what was going to happen to her when she arrived in London.

She set her lips firmly in an effort to stop them from trembling. 'What are your plans for me once we reach London, Monsieur le Duc? Am I to be locked up in chains until I reveal all to this man Maystone?' Considering she knew absolutely nothing about Helene Rousseau's plotting and planning, and so had nothing to reveal, that might possibly be for some considerable time.

'I did not—I will not allow anyone to "lock you up in chains", Lisette!' Christian huffed his impatience.

She gave a shrug of her shoulders. 'M'lord Maystone may have other ideas.'

Christian frowned his frustration for several moments, able to see the vulnerability in Lisette's eyes that she obviously thought to hide from him with the lashing of her tongue. Just as he recognised the stubborn set of her mouth for what it was—a determination on her part not to reveal that vulnerability.

He gave up any idea of having Lisette come to him and instead made the move to join her on the other side of the carriage. Movement, along with the jolting of the carriage, that caused him considerable pain but which he chose to ignore. He was more interested in Lisette's welfare than he was his own; he knew everything that had been revealed to her since they arrived in England must be more than a little frightening for her. Completely in character for the young woman he had come to know, she did not wish anyone to see that fear. Least of all, him.

Her eyes widened in alarm as she obviously guessed his intention. 'You must not—'

'I already am, my dear Lisette,' Christian assured her as he sank down gratefully onto the seat beside her before turning to take her in his arms. 'The "mountain" will happily come to you if you will not come to it,' he murmured ruefully. 'Lisette, *please*,' he cajoled as she struggled in his arms.

Lisette had no strength to remain immune

to the plea in Christian's voice, her shoulders dropping their defensive stiffness as she stopped fighting him and instead sank down against him, her head resting on his shoulder and so allowing her to hear the steady beat of his heart. 'I have done nothing wrong, Christian,' she said huskily.

His arms tightened about her. 'I know.'

'Do you?' She looked up at him.

'Yes.'

'How do you know?'

He gave a regretful grimace. 'By the fact that you really did not wish to travel to England with me, but came only for my comfort. By the fact that you most certainly did not wish to travel to London today.'

'That is true.' Lisette eyed him guardedly. 'But you did not seem to think that yesterday.'

'I have had a great deal of time to think since yesterday.' He sighed. 'Lisette, could we perhaps make ourselves more comfortable?'

'More comfortable?' she echoed doubtfully; she was already seated beside him and held in his arms; how much more 'comfortable' could they get inside a moving carriage?

'If I sit back this way, thus.' Christian moved so that his back was against the side of the coach rather than the back of the seat. 'Then I am able to do this, thus.' He manoeuvred his injured leg so that it lay along the length of the seat. 'And you can now sit, thus.' He turned Lisette so that she now sat along the length of the seat between his legs, her back resting against his chest, her feet on the seat and her knees drawn up, his arms about her waist.

A position Lisette was not at all sure to be proper, with so much of their bodies now in such close contact, particularly her bottom nestled back against the intimate vee between Christian's thighs.

She moistened her lips nervously. 'Christian…?'

'Are you about to deny me this simple pleasure, Lisette?' His voice was husky and extremely close to her ear.

Lisette was only too well aware that she was incapable of denying this man anything. It was part of the reason she had been so defensive on the journey from France to England, and for the time they had spent at the inn together. The same reason she had been so against accompanying him to London today.

Christian Seaton was not only the most handsome man she had ever seen, but also a duke, and a man whose service was valued by the English Crown.

A man far and above her own lowly station in life—the bastard daughter of a woman who owned and ran a French tavern. The same woman Christian knew to be plotting against his own Prince Regent, and who might be—no, in all probability was!—connected to the kidnapping of this man Maystone's young grandson.

The two of them sitting together so cosily in this carriage was ludicrous in those circumstances.

And yet...

Lisette was no longer an innocent when it came to a man's body, and she could now feel the undeniable hardness of Christian's lengthy arousal pressing against her.

His arms about her waist held her tightly back

against him, and his hands were resting dangerously close beneath the fullness of her breasts.

She moistened her lips. 'Christian, I do not think—'

'I do not want you to think, Lisette,' he groaned, his cheek now resting atop her head.

'But—'

'Shh,' he encouraged. 'We have been at odds with each other these past few days; let us now just sit here quietly and enjoy each other's company in silence.'

Lisette had no doubt that the now familiar tingling of her breasts and the almost uncomfortable warmth between her thighs was in direct response to Christian's close proximity. The hard arousal now pressing so insistently against the softness of her bottom was demonstration of Christian's response to that closeness.

Just as she had no doubt that it was not each other's 'company' they now wished to enjoy.

## Chapter Nine

Christian gave a sigh of contentment as he held Lisette in his arms once again and breathed in the familiar perfume of the softness of her hair, a heady mixture of lemon and the light scent of flowers. A perfume he had missed these past two days. As he had missed holding the sweet curves of her body pressed against his own.

Marcus had warned of it being a dangerous attraction yesterday evening, as the two men talked quietly and enjoyed a brandy together before retiring for the night.

Dangerous, and as undeniable to Christian as his next breath.

'What are you doing…?'

Christian laughed huskily. 'I do believe I am placing my hands upon your breasts.' His hands now cupped beneath that delicious fullness, allowing him to feel the hardened nipples pressing against his palms. Evidence that, no matter what she might now say to the contrary, Lisette enjoyed having her breasts held and fondled as much as he enjoyed holding them.

'The windows, Christian,' she protested half-heartedly. 'Anyone might ride by and see—and see what we are doing.'

Christian felt heartened by the 'we' in that statement. 'Pull down the blinds if it bothers you,' he encouraged softly as his lips now tasted the creaminess of her throat.

'Of course it bothers me—'

'Why?'

'I am not an exhibit for people to gawk at!'

'Then pull the damned blinds!'

'You are not well enough for such exertion.'

'Certain parts of my body appear to have other ideas.' He gave another husky chuckle. 'Does anything else about my intentions bother you?'

'I— Well—it is full daylight outside—'

'Pull down the blinds and it will not seem to be.'

'We really cannot, Christian.'

Christian could hear the lack of conviction in her breathy voice. 'Do it, Lisette, and you will see how easily we *can*,' he prompted more insistently, filled with an urgency to do more than fondle those full and tempting breasts.

He must indeed be feeling better.

These past few days had been a torment to him. Not because of his injury but because he had disliked intensely the distance that now lay between Lisette and himself, both emotionally and physically.

Here and now he wanted to dispense with that distance, to bare Lisette's breasts completely, pull on those roused nipples until they were as red as ripe strawberries, before taking them into his mouth and suckling. Deep and hard.

He smiled his satisfaction as Lisette moved up onto her knees on the seat to pull down first one blind and then another. 'If Monsieur le Duc should return—'

'Then he will know by the lowered blinds not to intrude,' Christian assured her softly.

She turned to look at him, eyes glittering in the now semi-darkness of the coach. 'Is that how you usually signal to each other that you are… engaged in such pursuits?'

'Hardly, when Marcus is married to my sister!' Christian drawled.

'I was referring to before he married your sister—'

'I believe you are deliberately trying to annoy me, Lisette.' Christian looked at her sternly. 'But, just so that we are clear on the subject, I do not make love to women in coaches. Ever. Does that satisfy your outraged sensibilities?'

She raised her brows. 'You have made love to me in a coach.'

'I will be putting you over my knee and spanking your bottom in a coach if you continue with this delaying tactic!' How could one tiny woman incite such desire within him and yet annoy him equally at the same time?

'Tactics are your forte, Christian.' Lisette pulled down the last of the blinds before once again turning to face him, chin lifted challengingly. 'And if you even attempt to spank my bottom, I will tell the Duke of Worthing and your sister, if I should meet her, what a brute you are!'

Christian gave an unconcerned grin.

He arched one blond brow. 'Unless I am mistaken, you now sound more curious at the prospect than distressed, Lisette…?'

She was. There was no denying it.

Having a man—Christian—spank her bottom sounded barbaric, and yet—

And yet…

If that was so, then why had the warm flush increased between her thighs and those already tingling buds that tipped her breasts become so hard and aching?

Unfortunately, her knowledge of physical pleasure was limited to these occasions with Christian, and so she could not answer that question.

She looked up at Christian through her lashes. 'Would you lift up my gown and remove my… my undergarments first, or spank me through my clothing?'

Just when Christian thought he might, for once, have the upper hand in a conversation with Lisette, she very neatly turned the tables on him in that totally disarming manner she had. 'Which do you think you would prefer?'

She appeared to give the matter some thought, arousing Christian even further. 'I do not believe such punishment would be as effective if administered through one's clothing. Do you?' she finally answered curiously.

Christian's lengthening manhood was now taking more than a passing interest in their conversation. 'Probably not,' he acknowledged gruffly. 'Perhaps we might carry out a little experiment on the matter…?'

Her eyes widened. 'Now?'

Unless he was mistaken, there was now an edge of anticipation in Lisette's tone. 'If that is what you would like?' He eyed her curiously.

He knew that some whores and courtesans enjoyed having their bottom spanked, as some gentlemen paid to administer such treatment. Behaviour which would no doubt have shocked their wives.

'Christian…?'

Lisette's eyes glowed a feverish blue in the semi-darkness of the carriage. With excitement? At the thought of Christian laying a hand on her bare bottom?

It was an intriguing and arousing thought.

'I believe I should enjoy…fondling your bare bottom rather than spanking it,' he ventured cautiously. He did not wish to misunderstand the situation; he knew better than most how heated Lisette's temper might be if he should proceed with a course of action she did not wish for.

His suggestion was answered with a slight lessening of that feverish glow in Lisette's eyes, but no less curiosity. 'Is that something that all men enjoy?'

The thought of any other man, singular or otherwise, touching any part of Lisette in pleasure or otherwise, was enough to cause Christian to want to forget the fondling and go straight to the spanking.

Besides which, he had no answer to her question; his own dealings with women these past fifteen years, in society or out of it, had been straightforward bed sport, enjoyable and satisfying, if not particularly memorable. Although he could not deny he had been tempted to put Lisette over his knee more than once for the rashness of her actions.

But surely it was the thin end of the wedge to indulge in such practices in bed?

*You are not in a bed but a carriage*, a little voice reminded inside his head.

Having started this conversation, was he not now duty-bound—?

Duty-bound be damned; having talked of the possibility, Christian now wanted Lisette over his knee, skirts thrown up, bottom bared, and once he had achieved that he could then decide what was best for the lady's pleasure as well as his own.

'Turn around so that I might unfasten and remove your gown.'

Lisette felt a delicious tremor of fear curl down the length of her spine as she heard the deep intensity of Christian's voice. At the same time she knew she had taken this conversation much further than she had intended.

At least she did not *think* she had intended it to go this far.

She had begun the conversation with the idea of shocking, only to have that audacity immediately turned back on her.

Her actions since first meeting Christian Seaton had not been at all how she would normally behave. He seemed to bring some devilment out of her which, once released, she did not seem to be able to take back under her control.

Added to which, Christian did not appear to be either surprised or shocked by her conversation. Indeed, that glitter of interest in his eyes seemed to be the same excitement as Lisette was now feeling.

She ran the moistness of her tongue across the sensitivity of her lips. 'I meant our conversation to be in the abstract only, Your Grace.'

'Liar.'

She was a liar, Lisette acknowledged slightly breathlessly. What had been intended to shock had now become completely, intimately personal.

She gave a shake of her head. 'I do not think I should like being spanked after all, Your Grace.'

He gave a hard smile. 'And perhaps that is the very reason that you need to be?'

She eyed him warily. 'I do not understand.'

'Turn around.'

'I—'

'I said turn around, Lisette.'

She swallowed at the implacability of his tone. 'I believe this was not such a good idea—'

'I am afraid you are a little too late in making that decision.'

Her heart fluttered in her chest. 'Too late…?'

'Turn,' he instructed again harshly.

At some time in their conversation, Lisette realised, she had ceased being the antagonist and instead had become the hunted. And in a confined space such as this carriage, she had nowhere to run or hide.

Except, perhaps, behind her earlier anger and indignation?

'Do not even attempt it, Lisette,' the Duke growled in warning. 'I was quite prepared to pass the time pleasantly on this journey to London, but instead I was first subjected to another of your lengthy and wholly undeserved rebukes, when it was Marcus who lifted you and put you in the carriage, not I. That was followed by another of your icy silences. I now believe you have traversed along a path from which there is no turning back.'

As Lisette had feared might be the case. 'I am overly impetuous sometimes, Your Grace—'

'It would seem that you are overly impetuous all the time, Lisette,' he corrected impatiently. 'A habit that needs to be curbed if we are to progress together.'

Lisette had no idea what *that* meant; there could not be much further to go on this journey to London, after which she was to be handed over to this man Maystone. She had no idea what was to become of her after that.

'Turn around, Lisette!'

She tensed at Christian's increasingly uncompromising tone, realising that she had pushed him too far with her taunting and curiosity, that there really was no 'turning back'.

She quickly turned her back towards him. 'You will not hurt me, Christian…?' she ventured nervously as she felt those deft fingers unfastening the tiny buttons at the back of her gown.

'I have not decided as yet,' he answered her gruffly.

Lisette did not move as the unfastened bodice of her gown slid down her arms before falling about her knees as she still knelt on the seat between his parted thighs, leaving her dressed only in her chemise, drawers, stockings and slippers.

'Now turn and face me.'

Lisette felt like a marionette as she slowly turned, face blazing with heat as Christian openly enjoyed staring at her breasts, the pleasurably hard pebbles of her nipples no doubt visible through the thin material of her chemise.

She wrapped her arms about her protectively. 'I am cold—'

'You are aroused,' Christian corrected huskily, 'which is not the same thing at all. Lower your arms, Lisette.'

She wanted to deny him, to berate him with her ready temper, but something in his eyes, a dark and unrelenting intensity, prevented her from doing so as she slowly, oh-so-slowly, lowered her arms instead.

'Now slip the straps of your chemise off your shoulders.'

Lisette gasped, even as she felt her breasts swell and tingle in response to the instruction. 'This cannot be at all correct, Christian— What is so funny?' she demanded as he chuckled throatily.

He gave a shake of his head. 'I do not believe you have done one "correct" thing since I first met you! Seeking me out in the darkness and coming back to my home with me. Running out into the street in the middle of the night, without hat or cloak, when you heard guns being fired.' His voice had hardened perceptibly. 'Driving my carriage as if you were born to it. Tending to not only my own wound but also Pierre's. Sailing on a boat back to England with me completely unchaperoned. Spending a night at an inn with me under the same circumstances. And now travelling in a coach alone with me—'

'That is most unfair!' Lisette protested. 'The circumstances under which we have so far been acquainted have not been conducive to—'

'I am known for my patience, Lisette—indeed, I believe I am praised far and wide for it,' Christian snapped impatiently. '*You*, however, have the ability to make me forget how to be patient, let alone behave the gentleman!' With this last comment he reached out to grasp the flimsy material of the neckline of her chemise and with one sharp pull ripped it from top to bottom.

'*Christian!*' Lisette's shocked gasp was accompanied by her raising her hands and placing them over her completely exposed breasts.

For once in their acquaintance Lisette was at a loss for words. Whether as the Comte de Saint-Cloud, the Duke of Sutherland or simply Christian, she did not appear to have any defences against this man.

'I can smell your arousal, Lisette,' he told her softly. 'Yes,' he insisted as she gasped in protest. 'Peaches, or perhaps apricots, mixed with a musky wholly feminine smell.'

'You would know of such things better than I!' she accused in an attempt to regain some of her lost dignity.

'Your insults do not bother me, Lisette,' Christian dismissed derisively. 'Not when I know they are made with the intention of annoying and distracting me.'

That *had* indeed been Lisette's intention. But this arrogant duke was obviously not going to allow himself to be distracted.

'Remove your hands, Lisette,' Christian bit out between his clenched teeth; he could not decide which was throbbing the most—his injured thigh because of these physical exertions, or the hardness of him. He did know that the heady smell of Lisette's arousal was causing him to fast lose all sense of control, let alone his usual veneer of civility. 'Now, Lisette!'

Her back straightened, her chin rising defensively. 'I am not a servant or a horse you may instruct to your will, Your Grace.'

'No—you are about to become my lover, which requires even more instruction from me, it seems!' Christian growled. 'And do not "Your Grace" me, Lisette, when you obviously have little or no respect for the title.'

A frown creased her brow. 'It is not my intention to be disrespectful.'

Christian sighed. 'It is not my intention to behave with disrespect towards you either. I am simply a man pushed beyond his limits.'

She eyed him warily even as her hands slowly lowered back down to her sides.

Christian's eyes had now completely adjusted

to the dim light of the carriage, allowing him to see the soft fullness of Lisette's naked breasts, tipped with fully engorged and pouting nipples, her waist incredibly slender before curving out to luscious hips. She wore white stockings held up by pretty white garters decorated with rose-buds the same deep fuchsia colour as her nipples.

'What do you *instruct* now, Christian?' She held herself proudly, shoulders back, breasts thrust forward.

He should never have started this, should not have allowed Lisette to challenge him so much that it was now almost too late for him to pull back from the brink— Damn it; it was too late! 'Help me to undress,' he encouraged huskily as he reached up and deftly removed the neck cloth from about his throat before unfastening his shirt.

Her throat moved as she swallowed. 'You intend to completely compromise me?'

He gave a hard, humourless grin. 'If that bothers you then we can always say that it was you who compromised me.'

'We will not need to say anything at all if you stop insisting upon this—this—'

'Lovemaking,' he supplied evenly.

'Lovemaking takes place between two people when they are married.'

'To each other?'

Another tirade of French insults—ones that Christian decided were best not translated—followed this remark.

'If not married, then at least in love with each other,' Lisette finally added primly.

Christian looked up at her through narrowed lids. 'How do you feel when I touch you here?' He reached out to push her ripped chemise completely aside before stroking his fingertips across the turgid tip of her breast, nodding his satisfaction as Lisette drew her breath in sharply, her back arching instinctively into that caress. 'Or do this?' He took her now fully erect nipple between his thumb and finger and gently squeezed, the scent of Lisette's arousal now so strong in the heaviness of the air Christian could almost taste it.

He *intended* to taste it before they reached London.

'I— That is—' Lisette now moved restlessly at the unfamiliar sensations coursing through her body. Unfamiliar before she had met Christian, that was.

No matter how angry she became with him, how uncertain she was about her future, this man only had to touch her with intimacy to arouse her. Sometimes he did not need to even touch her!

'Pleasurable,' Christian purred as he now cupped both her breasts in his hands.

'Yes…'

'Sensual.' The soft pads of his thumbs stroked across the swollen tips.

'Oh, yes…'

'Arousing.' He now pinched both those ripe berries between his thumbs and fingers.

'*Dieu*, yes!'

Christian proceeded to stroke and pinch, again and again, encouraged by Lisette's rapidly increasing breathing and the way she could not help but arch into those pleasurable caresses.

'Oh…!' she gasped within minutes. 'Do not stop. Oh, please do not, Christian…!' She pressed even harder into those caresses.

'I have no intention of doing so.' Christian frowned in concentration as he gauged exactly what gave her the greatest pleasure, determined to bring her to full pleasure before progressing any further.

The lightest of strokes. A caress. A gentle pinch. A squeeze, just so.

He had always been a considerate lover, he hoped, but it had never mattered quite so much to him before that the woman he was with attained the greatest pleasure from their lovemaking. He wanted Lisette to enjoy, to savour everything they did together, in the same way that he now was.

Lisette was beyond speech, beyond anything but the mindless pleasure flooding through her body, her breasts heavy and aching as Christian continued to stroke and squeeze. Between her thighs—*mon Dieu*, the swelling pleasurable sensation between her thighs was beyond anything she had ever experienced before.

'Let go, Lisette,' Christian encouraged fiercely, his face flushed, hair dishevelled.

'I do not under— Ooooh!' Something had burst free inside her, a huge explosion of such a myriad of pleasures, that overwhelming pulsing centred between her thighs, her core now contracting and releasing, throbbing as those waves of pleasure crashed over her again and again. 'Christian…!' she finally sobbed as she collapsed weakly forward against his chest.

Christian gathered Lisette into his arms, holding her close as he ran soothing hands up and down the length of her spine, allowing her to ride out the storm as she continued to softly gasp and sob in the aftershocks of her climax.

He felt such a swelling of emotions in his own chest as he continued to hold her, too many to be able to discern one from the other with any degree of certainty, but he knew he felt an increased tenderness, protectiveness towards the young woman he had just pleasured and now held in his arms. It was—

A sharp rap of knuckles sounded on one of the coach windows. 'We are almost arrived at

Sutherland House, Christian.' Marcus's voice was slightly muffled through the glass but the words were discernible nonetheless.

Christian barely had time to absorb those words, to register the sounds of the city outside—street vendors shouting their wares, the sounds of other carriages and horses traversing the cobbled streets, the ringing of church bells to the hour of twelve—sounds he had been totally unaware of until now, as he focused all of his attention on pleasuring Lisette.

Lisette pushed against his chest and sat up abruptly, eyes dark. Her cheeks were also flushed, her bared breasts full and the nipples red and swollen from Christian's ministrations.

She quickly grasped the two sides of her ripped chemise to cover those breasts as she glared at him accusingly.

'Do not,' Christian advised wearily as she opened those delectable lips to deliver what, he had no doubt, would be another sound tongue-lashing for the liberties he had just taken with her person.

Much as it might be deserved, it was not at all the tongue-lashing he now ached for.

And so much for *tasting* Lisette.

For having her taste him.

Christian had not realised how close to London they were when they began their lovemaking—it seemed he barely knew what time of day it was when he was with Lisette!—and he was now left feeling even more physically frustrated and out of sorts than he had been when they began.

A discomfort he would now have to deal with himself once he reached the privacy of his bedchamber at Sutherland House.

Speaking of which...

'You will need to dress, Lisette, if we are to arrive shortly—'

'How would you suggest I do that when my chemise is now ruined?' she came back agitatedly even as she moved along the seat before standing up, her crushed gown instantly falling to the carriage floor. 'Look at me!' She wailed her distress.

Christian *was* looking.

He could not seem to do anything else but

look as Lisette bent over slightly beneath the roof of the carriage, her hair in complete disarray, face flushed and wearing only the tatters of her ripped chemise, her drawers and those white stockings held up by the pretty garters.

She had the appearance of a sensual woman who had been well and truly seduced.

Which she was and had.

Never in Christian's experience had he ever known a woman to attain her physical release just from having her breasts played with.

'Christian!'

He blinked, shaking his head to clear it of such thoughts, as he raised his gaze from those responsive breasts to look at Lisette's face.

A face that bore an expression of dismay now, rather than her previous satiation, followed by agitation. 'Best to remove the chemise completely and I will dispose of it later,' he instructed economically. 'Then put your gown back on, your cloak over the top of it, and no one will be able to tell that you are not wearing your undergarment.'

'Until I remove the cloak,' she pointed out irritably even as she did as he suggested and impatiently removed the chemise.

A move that played havoc with Christian's unsatisfied arousal as he gazed his fill of slender shoulders, those completely bared breasts, her curvaceous waist and hips. 'Then do not remove your cloak until after you have reached the privacy of your bedchamber,' he answered her distractedly, the throb of his manhood painful still in its intensity.

'My bedchamber?' Lisette stilled, seemingly unconcerned with her near nakedness.

Would that Christian felt the same disinterest!

He nodded tersely. 'You will be staying with me at Sutherland House until…until I have opportunity to speak with Lord Maystone.'

'After which I am no doubt to be held a prisoner in the Tower of London, where all traitors to England are incarcerated.' Lisette's stubborn little chin rose. 'Whether they be innocent, as I am, or guilty,' she added disgustedly even as she pulled her gown into place to cover her nakedness.

'How you do love the dramatic, Lisette.' Christian snapped his impatience with the trait as he sat up and gingerly swung his legs to the floor of the carriage, paying special attention to his injured thigh. 'No one is going to lock you up in a tower, now or in the future.'

Lisette looked at him anxiously. 'You promise?'

Christian's expression softened as he saw the fear had returned to her eyes. 'I promise.'

Although he was not quite so confident about being able to keep that promise when the first person he saw as he stepped down from his carriage with Marcus's help was Lord Aubrey Maystone…

## Chapter Ten

*W*hat the devil—?

'My fault, I am afraid,' Marcus muttered after glancing at the older man coming down the steps towards them. 'I sent word ahead of the delay because of your having been shot, and to expect our arrival today. I also informed Maystone that you had not returned from France alone,' he added at Christian's scowl. 'I did not tell him that Lisette was Helene Rousseau's daughter—'

'I suppose I should be grateful for small mercies.' Christian continued to scowl his displeasure.

'I did so before I came to know Lisette for the charming girl she is,' he said defensively as Christian gave him a censorious frown.

'She is not a girl but a woman.'

'So it would seem.' Marcus gave a pointed glance towards the carriage. 'You obviously found her to be so on the journey here.'

'Marcus...' he growled in warning.

The other man shrugged. 'None of my business how and with whom you choose to pass the time of day, old chap.'

'I am pleased to hear it.' Christian turned to assist Lisette down from the carriage. 'Do not be alarmed,' he assured her gently as her panicked gaze moved past him to the rapidly approaching Aubrey Maystone. 'All will be well, Lisette.' He kept a firm hold of her arm, just in case she should be tempted to turn on her booted feet and run.

He would not put it past her to attempt such a move; Lisette had shown these past few days that she could be an enterprising young lady when the situation warranted it. And, damn it, her present apprehension in regard to Aubrey Maystone showed all the signs of becoming such a situation.

Maystone was usually the most charming of men, shrewd to a fault, admittedly, but invariably polite to the ladies. Unfortunately, this business with his grandson had turned even that amiable gentleman into a man intent on vengeance against the person or persons responsible for ordering the kidnapping. The three people now held in custody had only been instrumental in carrying out those orders; they had not instigated them.

Christian was certain that he now held the daughter of the person guilty of that crime close to his side. So close that he could feel the slight trembling of Lisette's body as she pressed against him, as if for protection.

His mouth tightened determinedly as he turned to greet the older man. 'Maystone.'

'Sutherland.' The other man nodded distractedly, his piercing gaze fixed on Lisette. 'Perhaps you would care to explain…?'

'I will make the introductions once we are inside.' Christian spared no time in waiting to see if the other two gentlemen agreed or disagreed with his suggestion as he stepped towards the house and took Lisette with him.

Whilst he had every reason to trust the members of his own household, he had no intention of engaging in any sort of conversation in a public street.

'He looks a very fierce gentleman,' Lisette commented softly after giving an anxious glance back at the two men following close behind them.

'He has…been under a great deal of strain these past few weeks,' Christian excused.

'How old is his grandson?'

'Just eight.'

*'Mon Dieu,'* she breathed softly. 'If Helene is guilty of ordering his kidnapping—'

'I believe that she is, yes,' Christian confirmed grimly.

She sighed heavily. 'Then once Lord Maystone knows the truth, he cannot help but feel it only just that Helene's child should be made to pay for her crimes. The "sins of the father" or, in this case, mother,' she added with a grimace.

'You cannot believe that any more than I,' Christian rebuked her.

She gave another of those Gallic shrugs. 'It is how I would feel if I were Lord Maystone.'

'Then I suggest you keep that opinion to yourself,' Christian came back with soft impatience as he turned to greet his butler. 'Miss Duprée would prefer to keep her cloak on for the moment, Evans,' he informed the elderly man as he reached to take the garment from her.

Lisette smiled her apology at the elderly butler even as her cheeks coloured a becoming pink.

No doubt at the memory of why she needed to continue to wear that cloak.

In truth, Christian felt slightly ashamed of his behaviour towards her in his carriage. He was a man usually in complete control, of himself as well as others, but where Lisette was concerned, it seemed he constantly lost every shred of that control.

And he defied anyone, least of all himself, to attempt to put any control on the stubbornly determined young lady he now knew Lisette to be...

'Refreshments in the library, if you please, Evans,' Christian instructed as he continued to limp his way into and through the cavernous entrance hall of his London residence.

Christian had chosen the library in which to talk, for two reasons.

Firstly, Lisette had found his house in France overwhelming and Sutherland House was even more so. The library was one of the less imposing rooms in the house, and the place where Christian usually spent his evenings at home relaxing by the fire, reading a book or dealing with correspondence.

His second reason—the library *was* his place of business, and he preferred any conversation with Aubrey Maystone to be completely that.

Despite Lisette's earlier observation, Christian believed the older man looked less strained than he had before Christian left for France. No doubt because he had now had the chance to enjoy the safe return and company of his only grandson, even if that abduction still played heavily on his mind.

Now all Christian had to do, once he had revealed Lisette's true identity, was to convince Maystone that she had no knowledge of or involvement in that kidnapping!

The first he would do carefully, so as not to

cause a reaction that would frighten Lisette any more. After which he would explain how Lisette had not even known Helene Rousseau was her mother until just a few short months ago.

Lisette waited only long enough for the butler to leave the room and close the door behind him before crossing to where Lord Maystone stood in front of the window looking out into the garden at the back of the house.

She drew in a deep breath, determined to have her say and not allow herself to be overwhelmed by this imposing house and its liveried servants. Or the three gentlemen with whom she shared the room. Although that was a little harder to do when two of them were dukes and the third a lord.

Lisette straightened her shoulders determinedly. 'I cannot tell you how sorry I am for all that you have endured, m'lord.' That gentleman's eyes widened in obvious surprise, no doubt because she spoke to him in French as she reached out and took both of his hands in her own. 'Your grandson has not suffered any lasting effects from his ordeal, I hope?' she prompted anxiously.

'Good Lord, Sutherland, she's French!' the older man gasped, obviously shocked.

'I have often remarked upon Maystone's powers of observation, have I not, Christian?' Marcus Wilding drawled from where he had made himself comfortable in a chair beside the lit fireplace.

'Now is not the time for levity, Marcus,' Christian warned.

'I am indeed French, m'lord, and my name is Lisette Duprée.' She gave a small curtsy as she continued to concentrate on the man before her rather than the conversation of the two gentlemen behind her. 'I am also—'

'My ward,' Christian put in hastily.

'Your ward…?' Lord Maystone echoed faintly, appearing totally bewildered by these introductions.

As no doubt he was. That explanation might have sufficed in a Portsmouth inn, but Lisette doubted very much that any in London would believe Christian's insistence in introducing her as such.

Her mouth firmed. 'I am also—'

'Lisette, no!' Christian attempted to forestall her. 'Let me—'

'—Helene Rousseau's illegitimate daughter.' Lisette refused to be silenced, having no intention of attempting to hide her identity or deceive the gentleman now standing before her.

'Good God…!' Lord Maystone stared at her in astonishment.

'I do not think God has, or ever had, any part in Helene Rousseau's actions.' Lisette wrinkled her nose disapprovingly. 'I can only offer my most sincere regret for any hurt or discomfort she may have caused to you or your family.'

Lisette's candour had completely overridden Christian's own intention, of approaching the subject of Lisette's identity as Helene Rousseau's daughter with caution. Indeed, he had been rendered momentarily speechless by Lisette's disarming honesty.

As Worthing and Maystone were similarly

struck, if the looks on those two gentlemen's faces were any indication.

It was a candour which Christian should no doubt have taken into account when deciding upon his own plan of action in regard to revealing Lisette's identity.

'Bravo, Lisette.' Worthing was the first to recover from his shock, as he gave her a gentle and appreciative clap. 'She has the courage of ten men, Christian,' he added admiringly.

'It takes no courage at all to tell the truth, Your Grace.' Lisette was the one to answer him ruefully.

'It does, in my experience.' Marcus grimaced.

'And mine,' Christian added softly, finding himself once again admiring and not a little in awe of Lisette's determination to be truthful. Even if, in this case, he might have wished her to be a little less so. 'I believe you may safely allow me to deal with any further explanations, Lisette—'

'Helene Rousseau's daughter!' Maystone appeared to have recovered his voice, although he continued to stare at Lisette as if he had seen a ghost, seeming unaware that Lisette still held on to his hands.

'Illegitimate daughter,' Lisette corrected firmly.

'I— But—' Maystone gave a shake of his head as if to clear it. 'Helene Rousseau does not have a daughter.'

'I was as surprised as you obviously are when she claimed me as such only a few months ago,' Lisette asserted regretfully. 'You cannot know how much I have wished since that it was not the case,' she added heavily.

Lisette had resisted that connection from the start. She also felt heartily ashamed of any part Helene might have played in the kidnapping of an innocent eight-year-old boy.

But, having now met Lord Maystone, Lisette felt a renewed anger towards the older woman. It was bad enough that Helene had abandoned her own child to be brought up by strangers, but Helene's crime against Lord Maystone and his family, because of her political machinations—and a crime she had given no indication of caring about these past months—was truly unforgivable.'

Lisette gave Lord Maystone's hands an empathetic squeeze. 'I can only apologise again and state how sorry I am for the pain and distress that has been caused to you and your family.'

'Sutherland…?'

Christian had every sympathy with Maystone's slightly dazed expression; Lisette had the same effect on him. Often. 'It is quite true, I assure you,' he confirmed. 'But I also want you to know that I have brought Lisette to England with me for her own protection. Let me assure you she had no knowledge of or involvement in your grandson's kidnapping,' he added just as firmly.

'I do not— This is—' Maystone still seemed at a complete loss for words as he dropped down onto the upholstered window seat as the butler entered with the refreshments, none in the room speaking again until after that elderly gentleman had departed.

Lisette sat down on the seat next to Maystone. 'Unfortunately, as I have found, my birthright does not become any easier to comprehend or accept with time.'

'Would you care to do the honours, Lisette?' Christian indicated the tea tray as a way of changing the subject and easing some of the tension in the room.

She gave him an impatient glance. 'Could you see to it, Christian? Can you not see I am still busy attempting to commiserate with Lord Maystone?'

Christian heard Marcus's guffaw of laughter behind him. Indeed, he had to bite the inside of his own cheeks to stop himself from laughing. Maystone appeared to still be suffering from the shock of Lisette's earlier revelation, this latest social gaffe seeming to pass him by.

'Did I say something amusing?' Lisette frowned her irritation with Marcus's laughter.

Marcus straightened in his seat, still grinning. 'It is only—'

'It is only that I thought you might enjoy pouring the tea,' Christian cut in smoothly.

'Because I am a woman?' Lisette gave a disgusted snort to accompany her dismissive comment. 'Why should I pour your tea for you and your friends when you are more likely to be acquainted with how they take their tea than I am?'

It was a good point, Christian acknowledged. Except he didn't, of course, never having poured tea in his privileged life before, for his friends or himself. Which was no reason for him not to do so now. Although Maystone, for one, looked in need of something stronger than tea.

'I will pour you a cup of tea, Lisette.' Christian proceeded to do so, much to the amusement of his brother-in-law. 'But I think the gentlemen would prefer brandy…?'

'Just a small one,' Marcus accepted drily. 'Then I must hurry home to Julianna.'

Christian was well aware of the fact that it was only Marcus's fascination as to what Lisette would do or say next which had prevented him from departing already.

He finished pouring the tea and carried the cup and saucer across the room to place it on the table beside Lisette; having observed her at breakfast this morning, he knew it was exactly as she liked it—milk and a little sugar. 'Maystone?' he prompted sharply. Really, the news of Lisette being Helene Rousseau's illegitimate daughter was surprising, yes, but not *so* shocking that the older man should still be rendered speechless.

'Hmm? Oh. Yes. Thank you, Sutherland.' Maystone nodded, still staring at Lisette in that bemused fashion. 'A brandy would be most welcome.'

'I do not believe you should be drinking strong liquor when you are injured, Christian.' Lisette frowned her disapproval as she watched him pour the amber liquid into three glasses before handing two of them to his guests and retaining one for himself.

Christian heard Marcus give another muffled laugh. A laugh his friend tried—and failed—to hide behind a look of innocence when Christian narrowed his gaze on him. Lord knew what Marcus would report back to their mutual friends concerning his friendship with Mademoiselle Lisette Duprée. They were not even married and she was leading him about by the nose—

*Married?*

Where on earth had *that* come from?

Wherever it had come from, it could go back again! He had never met a more opinionated, irritating, bossy, *infuriating* young woman in his life than Lisette Duprée.

*Or one quite so desirable.*

Well, yes, there was that, and he really should not have taken things as far as he had in the carriage. Even so, desire did not make up for the fact that Lisette was also—also—

What else was she?

Alone and defenceless.

Apart from that sharp tongue!

Vulnerable and frightened.

Again, apart from that sharp tongue!

She was also about to be used in a game of political chess for which she bore no responsibility or knowledge, but might nevertheless be the one called upon to pay the highest price.

Even that sharpness of Lisette's tongue and intelligence of mind could not save her if that should prove to be the case.

But Christian had just realised a way in which he might do so…

If *he* was prepared to pay the price.

Many families in English society were related to or married into the French aristocracy.

Which Lisette most certainly was not. Instead, she was the illegitimate daughter and niece of two notorious French spies.

Maybe so, but no one chose where and to whom they would be born. Lisette was a victim of her own circumstances, not a perpetrator of them—

Good God, he could not seriously be contemplating doing the unthinkable?

'Christian…?' Marcus prompted sharply. 'I believe you are about to spill your brandy all over the carpet!'

He looked blankly at the man he had known since childhood, his thoughts still too onerous for him to form a sensible or coherent reply.

Was he really prepared to go as far as *that* in order to keep his promise to protect Lisette? For there was no doubting that no one would dare to arrest or harm the Duchess of Sutherland—

'You see.' Lisette stood up to briskly cross the room before plucking the brandy glass from

Christian's relaxed fingers. 'I said that you should not attempt to drink brandy in your already weakened state.' She tutted disapprovingly as she placed the glass down on Christian's desktop.

His heavy oak antique desk that had once belonged to a king.

Christian, however, was not the King of England, and if he did decide to tie himself to Lisette Duprée, then he knew it would be for life.

A life spent with an impulsive and totally irrepressible woman who would make a terrible duchess.

'Are you about to take me away and lock me in a cell, m'lord?' Lisette spoke to Maystone with her usual directness.

That gentleman looked startled by such a suggestion. 'I— Why, no, I had not thought of doing such a thing.'

'Why not?'

'I— Well—' Maystone gave a shake of his head. 'I have no evidence— I trust Sutherland's word if he has vouched for you.'

'He has,' Christian asserted sharply, although

he could not help but feel surprised that Maystone had ceded his ground so easily.

Indeed, Maystone still looked befuddled, clearly as disconcerted by Lisette's directness as the next man. And Christian, as the *next man*, was highly disconcerted by her!

Maystone nodded. 'I really need time to consider this…situation before taking any further action.'

'Then perhaps you two gentlemen have visited long enough for today,' Lisette now told Worthing and Maystone politely but firmly. 'Christian is weakened still and needs to rest after his long journey.'

What Christian *needed* was to retake charge in his own household and not have it, and him, dictated to by a mere chit of a girl—

'I believe you are right.' Maystone downed the last of his brandy before rising quickly to his feet and placing his empty glass down on the desk beside Christian's.

Good God, they were all doing it now!

It really was insupportable that Christian's life, his very existence, most certainly the authority he had possessed since birth, was being eroded in just minutes by this bossy and opinionated French miss.

'I shall come back and…and discuss this further in the morning, Christian, once I have had chance to ponder the situation,' Maystone added distractedly.

As far as Christian was concerned, Maystone could 'ponder' all he liked and it would not change the outcome; *he* could not allow Lisette to come to any harm. Indeed, the mere thought of it caused a cold shiver down the length of his spine.

'Mademoiselle Duprée.' Maystone now nodded abruptly. 'Worthing?'

'Definitely time we were leaving.' Marcus nodded after a single glance at the thundercloud he no doubt saw forming on Christian's brow. 'I shall bring Julianna to see you tomorrow morning, Christian.'

After he had no doubt regaled Christian's young sister with all the details of his relationship with Lisette. Including what Marcus suspected might have happened in the carriage on their way from Portsmouth to London; as far as Christian could see, the married couple kept no secrets from each other.

He also knew instinctively that his sister was sure to like Lisette, if only for the fact that she appeared to have taken charge of Christian and his household without so much as a by-your-leave.

'There is no rush for you to leave now,' he assured his brother-in-law hastily. 'Indeed, I was about to suggest that perhaps you might care to take Lisette home to Worthing House with you, so that you and Julianna might act as chaperone—'

'I am not in need of a chaperone—'

'But of course you are, my dear.' Maystone spoke up bravely over Lisette's outraged protest. 'A single unmarried lady does not reside in a single gentleman's house without a chaperone, even that of her guardian.' He gave a slightly bewildered shake of his head. 'Forgive me, Sutherland, I was—I am still—a little shocked to learn of Miss Duprée's...lineage.'

'*Half* my lineage,' Lisette cut in dismissively. 'I

fear my father's identity is unknown, and likely to remain so,' she informed him at his questioning look.

'Oh. Well. Yes.' Maystone looked more disconcerted than ever. No doubt at hearing Lisette speaking so frankly of her illegitimacy.

'And I do not intend going anywhere, Christian.' She turned back to him. 'Now that I *am* here—' she gave him a glowering look '—I intend to continue seeing that all my good work of these past three days does not become undone simply because you are too stubborn to call for a doctor.'

'And if I now agree to send for the physician?' Christian challenged.

'Then I still could not leave you here without family or friend to attend you,' she maintained obstinately.

Christian looked at her searchingly, sensing—sensing—ah, yes, there it was—a telltale glitter of tears in those deep blue eyes.

Because he was attempting to save Lisette's reputation by sending her to stay with his sister and brother-in-law?

Admittedly, it would also save his own reputation, but—

There was no *but* to this situation, he conceded heavily; Lisette was the one without family or friends, apart from himself, and to send her away, albeit to stay with his sister and Marcus, would be the height of cruelty after all that she had done for him.

'It was merely a thought, Lisette.' He sighed in defeat. 'Of course, if you wish to stay here at Sutherland House, then you must do so.'

She blinked, lashes slightly dampened by those tears she was determined not to allow to fall. 'If Lord Maystone does not wish to take me away for questioning as yet, then yes, I do prefer to stay here.'

'Then it is settled.' Christian braced his shoulders before turning to Marcus and Maystone. 'Gentlemen?'

Marcus rose elegantly to his feet. 'I have no doubt you do need to rest following the…the exertions of the journey here, Christian,' he added drily.

Pointedly, Christian acknowledged irritably,

knowing full well to what 'exertions' Marcus was referring. As did Lisette, by the becoming blush that had now coloured her cheeks. Maystone still looked befuddled.

And perhaps Christian *did* need to rest; his thoughts of a few minutes ago regarding marriage to Lisette certainly indicated that he was not in his right mind!

It seemed that he was to have Lisette as his guest at Sutherland House after all. And he had not had to fight Aubrey Maystone, verbally or otherwise, in order to achieve it.

His gaze narrowed on the older man as he continued to stare at Lisette as if she were an apparition.

What was wrong with the man?

Perhaps his grandson's kidnapping had affected Maystone more seriously than any of them had suspected?

But, if that was so, then why was he not insisting on taking Lisette into his custody?

He felt a throbbing behind his eyes, as indication that so much thought—and so many unanswered questions—had resulted in him developing a headache. 'Just so,' he now answered Marcus vaguely. 'Do not visit with Julianna too early tomorrow morning, Marcus,' he added wearily as he rang for Evans to show the gentlemen out. 'I have a feeling I will not be at my best until later in the day.'

Marcus's dark brows rose. 'You know your sister almost as well as I; it will be as much as I can do to prevent her from visiting you later today once she knows you are returned from France and injured!'

Yes, Christian did know Julianna very well. He also knew that she had Marcus entwined about her little finger.

'Then I suggest you do not tell her I am injured,' he bit out. 'As to the rest, I am sure you will manage to think of some other manner in which to divert her,' he added ruefully.

Worthing gave a devilish grin. 'I shall do my best.'

Lisette was very aware of Lord Maystone's gaze still fixed upon her as the two gentlemen prepared to leave. No doubt his decision not to arrest her as yet was only because he was still trying to come to terms with the fact that his enemy's illegitimate daughter now stood just feet away from him.

Having now met Lord Maystone, Lisette felt even more ashamed of her connection to Helene Rousseau. The woman was a monster beyond her imagining, to have instigated the kidnapping of this man's young grandson.

She also could not deny the heaviness she felt in her chest at Christian's obvious effort to send her away to stay at his sister's home. Evidence, no doubt, that now he was back in his own household, and despite his earlier promise to protect her, he wanted to be rid of her.

## Chapter Eleven

'Do you have everything you need?'

Lisette turned at the open doorway from the hallway into the comfortable bedchamber she had been shown into by the butler just minutes ago, on Christian's instructions.

That same gentleman now leaned against the door frame, looking across the room at her as she sat on the side of the four-poster bed that dominated the luxuriously appointed cream-and-gold room.

A bedchamber fit for a princess.

Or a duchess…

Christian Seaton's duchess.

Except he did not appear to have one of those.

Lisette wondered why that was when he was a

handsome man in his early thirties and in possession of a wealth she could only ever dream about.

But perhaps he considered his work for the English Crown too dangerous to risk taking a wife? The fact that Christian had been shot only days ago would seem to confirm it *was* dangerous work.

And the truthful answer to his question was that she did not have *anything* she 'needed'. No home. No money. Her future uncertain. No kind relatives to whom she might ask for help.

She felt wholly disconnected from any and everything that was familiar to her, and her earlier bravado upon arriving at this imposing residence had now totally deserted her.

Added to, she had no doubt, by the memory of Christian's efforts to rid himself of the responsibility of her just a short time ago…

'I believe so, thank you,' she answered Christian in a subdued voice.

'You do not sound as if you do.' Christian favoured his left leg as he stepped further into the room.

Evidence that he was once again in pain?

Lisette stood up. 'Do you wish me to inspect and re-dress your wounds before you retire to your bedchamber?'

'No, thank you,' Christian refused ruefully. He was only too well aware of what that 'inspection' might lead to, despite his disquieting thoughts of earlier and the discomfort of his wound.

A certain part of his anatomy did not seem to give a damn about either of those things and leaped up eagerly in response to Lisette's slightest touch. The very reason he had chosen to leave the bedchamber door open when he entered.

'What am I to do whilst you are resting?' There was a frown between Lisette's eyes.

*Stay out of trouble* was Christian's first thought, followed by the knowledge that it would be no good to instruct Lisette to do any such thing when trouble, of one sort or another, seemed to follow her around.

Not particularly through any fault of her own, he accepted; Miss Lisette Duprée just seemed to be a magnet for all things troublesome.

'Perhaps you might also rest?' he suggested mildly, determinedly walking over to the winlow to look down into the square below rather han at Lisette; she looked so woebegone at the moment, it was all he could do not to take her into his arms and offer her comfort.

A comforting that he had no doubt would lead to the deeper intimacy between them that he was trying so hard to avoid now that they were in his London home. For Lisette's sake; all servants gossiped, even if one might wish they did not, and London society was so quick to condemn when it came to the reputation of a lady, no matter how much Christian might continue to publicly claim that Lisette was his ward.

Damn both Marcus and Maystone; one for ignoring his obvious request for assistance, the other for being so befuddled of wits he had not only seemed, but had proved to be, incapable of any action or sensible thought where Lisette was concerned.

Not that Christian would have allowed the older man to take Lisette away with him. He could not have allowed that after his earlier promises, but he could have done with a *little* assistance from one or both of the other gentle-men in regard to this situation.

A situation not of Lisette's choosing, he once again reminded himself heavily.

'I am not tired,' she answered him huskily.

Christian frowned now at the way Lisette kept her face turned away from him. Damn it, if she was crying…!

He was weakened and felt as much at a loss as most men did when confronted by a woman's tears. The more so if they were Lisette's—she had been so stalwart in her behaviour and ac-tions up until now. He could not think of many women who would have acted as bravely as she had done these past few days—escaping out of windows in order to warn him of danger, com-ing to his rescue after he had been shot, leav-ing behind her home and country to sail all the way to England to care for him on the journey.

And her reward? She had been bundled into a coach and brought to London against her will. Moreover, she had been made love to in that coach by the very man who was responsible for her present dilemma.

Perhaps, in the circumstances, Lisette was allowed to shed a few tears.

'Come here.' Christian limped across the room to sit down on the bed beside her and take her into his arms. 'No, do not fight me, Lisette,' he soothed gently as she did exactly that. 'Let me hold you,' he encouraged gruffly.

'Why?' Her voice was muffled against his chest as his arms held her too tightly for her to escape.

'Why what?' Christian allowed himself the pleasure of winding one of her silky curls about his finger.

'You so obviously wanted either Le Duc or m'lord to take me away earlier!' she accused brokenly as she finally gave up the fight and her head rested against his chest.

Yes, there were definitely tears, Christian acknowledged as he felt their damp heat soaking the front of his shirt. And not for any of the reasons he had attributed, but because *he* had hurt her feelings earlier. 'I thought only of your reputation,' he soothed, knowing he was not being altogether truthful.

He *had* been concerned with Lisette's reputation, but more so with his inability to resist her.

Good Lord, when he had made love to her in his carriage earlier today, he had not given a care for where they were or that his leg pained and discomforted him. How much less resistance would he have against her once he was completely well again? Even now he was totally aware of the fact that there was only the thin material of her gown between his hands and the bareness of her creamy skin. A fact made possible by his having ripped her chemise to shreds earlier in a fit of passion.

He had never behaved in such a rough and demanding manner with any woman before Lisette.

Had never burned so deeply with lust before Lisette.

She gave a choked laugh now. 'I have no reputation left to lose, Christian.'

'Of course you do. When this is over—'

'I will still be a stranger in a strange land, with no money or family, and the illegitimate daugh-

ter of a French tavern owner who is an enemy
of your country.'

Christian gave a wince at this unflatteringly
accurate description of Lisette's circumstances.

'I know I have previously spoken to the contrary, but…once Lord Maystone realises that I
truly do not know anything about my—about
Helene Rousseau's plots and plans, perhaps you
might consider taking me as your mistress?' Lisette looked up at him with tear-damp eyes.

*'What?'*

'Until such time as you take a duchess, of
course,' she added hastily, no doubt at his hor-
rified expression. 'I should not like to intrude
upon a marriage.'

If Christian had been startled by her outspokenness to Maystone earlier, he now found himself completely stunned by Lisette's suggestion
of becoming his mistress.

Women simply did not behave in this forward
manner—

He already knew that Lisette was not like other
women. Indeed, he had never met another like

her. Innocent on the one hand, completely practical on the other.

But not so innocent that she did not know that she had only one thing that was truly her own, and practical enough to decide to whom and when she would give it.

'Have you forgotten your claim—"I would rather sell my soul to the devil than be beholden to you for a moment longer"?' He huskily reminded her of the insult she had hurled at him during their heated exchange at the inn yesterday.

If Lisette telling him exactly what she thought of him and his having had no choice but to listen to those thoughts could be called an *exchange*!

'I have said that I do.'

'But you have now changed your mind?'

'Do not mock me, Christian.' Lisette did not appreciate his levity when she had spent the past few minutes considering her future.

She had no real wish to return to France, now that she had been made aware of the full extent of Helene's actions. Indeed, it might be dangerous for her to do so.

But if she was allowed to remain free and in England, then her lack of spoken English would limit her options of employment. Something she intended to rectify as soon as possible, but unfortunately, that would not be soon enough for her to become a companion, governess or even a maid in an English household.

But if she had no choice but to become some rich gentleman's mistress, then she would rather make the choice of that lover for herself. She already knew that she and Christian were physically compatible. Much better, if she had to become some man's mistress, that she at least enjoy the gentleman's attentions.

'Besides, I should not be beholden to you,' she reasoned briskly. 'You would set me up in my own small establishment, and in exchange I would make myself available to you whenever you wish it. That is the way these things are arranged, is it not?' she added with a pragmatism she was not sure she actually felt as yet but hoped to achieve, and certainly now wished to convey to Christian.

The Duprées had been great believers in pragmatism; they had often had need to be on the farm, when the crops had failed or the cows did not provide enough milk to sell.

A pragmatism Lisette was sorely in need of when all she possessed, besides herself, were the few belongings Christian had purchased for her before leaving Paris.

'I have no need of a mistress.'

She looked up at him sharply. 'Is that because you already have one?'

'No, of course I do not—' He broke off in obvious exasperation. 'Lisette, you cannot just offer to become a man's mistress without his first having given indication that is what he wants too!'

Her eyebrows rose. 'Earlier today in your carriage was not an indication of your desire for me?'

'Well. Yes.' He gave an impatient shake of his head. 'Of course it was an *indication* that I desire you, but I— Lisette, I have never set myself up with a mistress—'

'Why not?'

'—and I do not intend to start now. What do you mean—why not?' He scowled darkly.

She gave a shrug. 'I thought all society gentlemen, most especially a duke, took a mistress?'

'Then you thought wrong.' He glowered. 'Neither I nor, to my knowledge, any of my close friends have ever done so.'

'That does not mean you could not do so now.' It was not an ideal situation for Lisette either, nor had it been an easy decision for her to make, but she really did have so very few choices left to her. Once she had told Lord Maystone what she knew—which was very little, and most certainly did not include Helene caring for her enough to respond to blackmail on her behalf—then it was easy to surmise that neither he nor Christian would have any further use for her.

Unless she were to offer her services in some other way.

'I do *not* have need of a mistress,' Christian bit out between gritted teeth.

'Well, certainly not now, when you are incapacitated—'

'Ever!'

'There is no need to shout, Christian—'

'No need to—!' His arms moved from about

her before he stood up to glower down at her even more darkly. 'There is every reason to shout when you have just offered to become my mistress.'

'An offer you have clearly refused.' Lisette stood up, chin raised proudly. 'Which means I will have to find some other acceptable gentleman to whom I might—'

'You will do no such thing!'

She gave a wince. 'You are still shouting, Christian.'

'I am about to put you over my knee and administer that spanking we discussed earlier if you do not cease talking of this subject—' He broke off as Evans appeared in the open doorway, accompanied by a wide-eyed maid carrying a pitcher and several towels.

Lisette was unsure who was the most embarrassed: herself for having had Christian's threat to spank her bottom overheard—and possibly some of the conversation leading up to that threat?—or the two shocked servants at being the ones to have overheard that threat.

Christian glared furiously.

'I… I thought Miss Duprée might care for some hot water and towels with which to refresh herself after your journey, Your Grace.' Evans was the first to recover, his expression once again respectfully deadpan.

The situation was so ludicrous, Lisette acknowledged as her initial dismay began to recede, that it was all she could now do to stop herself from laughing. Her efforts not to do so were not helped by the continuing look of outrage on Christian's face.

He breathed in deeply—fighting for control?— before answering his butler tautly. 'Leave them and go.'

'Thank you, Evans,' Lisette managed to add in heavily accented English, with the addition of a smile, in the hope of making up for Christian's abruptness; it was very kind of the butler to have thought of her comfort in that way.

'Close the door on your way out,' Christian instructed stiffly once the pitcher of water and towels had been placed on the washstand.

Christian considered it shocking enough that Lisette had offered to become *his* mistress, but the idea that she might so much as think of making that same scandalous offer to another gentleman was even more unacceptable.

He would rather accept the offer himself than—

*No!*

He was not going to take Lisette as his mistress or anything else. Once the situation with Maystone had been settled then Christian would do everything in his considerable power to help Lisette to find gainful employment. Legitimate gainful employment. In a respectable household. Many women in English society now had French maids, *emigrées* from the years of upheaval in France, and although Lisette might be a little outspoken for such a post, he was sure that Julianna, if she had no need of her services herself, might at least be able to advise the younger woman on how best to behave.

And maybe, from time to time, the two of them might meet, have luncheon or afternoon tea together, so that Christian might see Lisette, talk with her and ascertain that she was happy and being well cared for—

A duke did not have luncheon or afternoon tea with a lady's maid.

Well. No. Perhaps not.

There was no *perhaps* about it; it simply was not done.

Then perhaps Julianna might be persuaded to invite the two of them—

He was taking himself round and round in circles, Christian realised. And Lisette stood at the centre of all of them.

If—when Lisette eventually left his household and became a lady's maid, or perhaps just a maid, then he must accept that he would not be able to see her again.

The thought did not sit well with him.

He could not imagine being unable to look into those beautiful blue eyes or to see the spark of anger that so often lit them. Or to listen to her outrageous conversation; even her scoldings were so much more entertaining than anything any other woman had ever said to him.

As for the effect she had upon him physically…

She had, Christian realised, made a place for

herself in his life these past few days. A place that no other woman ever had.

A place that would gape like an open wound once Lisette was no longer there to fill it.

Meaning what?

*That he had to be suffering a fever of some kind—perhaps his wound had become infected after all?—if he was once again considering doing the unthinkable!*

He straightened. 'I am sure we will both feel… calmer, more able to discuss your future, once we have rested after our journey.'

Lisette could not see that there was anything more for them to discuss on the subject when she had already considered her future from all angles.

Christian had just refused the obvious choice.

She had no skills, except those of working on a farm or in a tavern. If the English taverns were anything like the one owned by Helene Rousseau, then she was more likely than not, as an unprotected young woman in a strange country, to end up one night with her skirts up to her waist and her virtue lost.

No, better by far to choose that life for herself, to choose the man for herself, rather than have it chosen for her by some unwashed lout in a dark alley.

She stood up. 'You are right, of course, Christian. As usual,' she added tightly.

Christian eyed her guardedly; an acquiescent Lisette was decidedly more worrying than the virago Lisette. 'What are you up to…?'

She opened wide eyes. 'What does this mean—"up to"?'

Christian wished he felt reassured by those innocent wide blue eyes. Unfortunately, they had the opposite effect; when Lisette looked innocent then he could be sure she was about to do something she should not.

He sighed. 'In your case it means—what are you plotting and planning to do this afternoon, while I am resting, that you should not be doing?'

She shrugged. 'I have no idea what you are talking about.'

Yes, definitely plotting and planning… 'You realise you cannot leave here, Lisette?' He watched her closely. 'That to do so would be dangerous?'

Her chin rose. 'For whom?'

Christian frowned his irritation. 'For you, of course. England is rife with French spies— This is not funny, Lisette.' His frown turned to a scowl.

'Of course it is.' She continued to chuckle. 'I am not safe in France; I am not safe in England. Where shall I be safe, Monsieur le Duc?'

*With him*, Christian instantly answered, and then just as quickly dismissed it again. Lisette was *not* safe with him, or *from* him; he had more than proved that in the coach earlier.

He gave a weary shake of his head. 'I am too tired to argue with you just now, Lisette. Only give me a few hours to sleep and I promise I will be rested enough for you to argue with for as long as you wish to do so.'

'I do not argue with you—'

'You do nothing else!' Christian's voice rose, this time impatiently. 'You are the most contrary woman— I swear that if I said the sky is blue that you would argue it was pink.'

She wrinkled her pretty nose. 'Sometimes it is. Have you never seen the sunset when—?'

'I am going to bed, Lisette,' he announced flatly as he walked determinedly across the room to the door. 'Try to behave yourself in my absence.'

Lisette kept her chin raised high until Christian had left the bedchamber and then, only then, did she allow her shoulders to droop dejectedly.

She had buried all her scruples, her dreams for the future, had done the unthinkable and offered to become Christian's mistress, and he had rejected the idea totally. There had not been the slightest hesitation or doubt. He did not want her.

He could not have told her any more clearly that she had only been an amusement to him in Paris, a diversion on the journey here, one he did not need or want now that he was back in London and was once again every inch the Duke of Sutherland.

'What do you mean she went out, Evans?' Christian demanded. 'Where did she go? And when?'

His butler looked distinctly uncomfortable.

'Miss Duprée went out for a walk, possibly two hours ago, Your Grace.'

'Where?' he repeated forcefully, hands clenched into fists at his sides.

Christian really had been exhausted by the time he had reached his own bedchamber earlier, and he had not even bothered to undress before dropping weakly down on top of the bed and falling into a deep sleep.

His valet had woken him several hours later, armed with a cup of tea to refresh him and hot water in which to bathe. Christian had enjoyed the luxury of the latter long after his valet had completed his shave and the bath water had become cold.

The bandage on his thigh had come off quite easily after his soak in the bath, and he was relieved to see that the wound was healing well once he had removed the soiled bandage upon stepping from the bath. He had also managed to reapply a fresh bandage himself; he certainly did not need any gossip below stairs concerning how he had acquired such a wound.

Once he was dressed he had gone downstairs

in search of Lisette, only to be told that she was not there. Which had the effect of completely undoing all the good work of the previous hours of sleep, followed by the relaxation in the bath.

It was also in complete opposition to what Christian had instructed before going to his bed-chamber.

He really was going to have to put Lisette over his knee and spank her—

'There was something of a...language barrier, Your Grace, but I believe she did not intend to be out long,' his butler answered uncomfortably.

There would be no 'language barrier' nec-essary once Christian caught up with Lisette. 'Language' would not be used, but physical ret-ribution.

'To be truthful, Your Grace, I was becoming a trifle worried about her myself,' Evans con-tinued awkwardly. 'I had assumed she was just going to walk about the square, but she has been gone far too long for that to be the case. A young lady out alone...' The elderly butler broke off with a wince as Christian gave him a glower-ing frown.

Although in truth, he could not hold any of his household responsible for Lisette's actions; she was impulsive and strong-willed to the point where she was a danger to herself and everyone else. Christian could not deny that her impulsiveness and strong will had saved his life a time or two, but he had been perfectly serious earlier when he had warned Lisette of the dangers lurking beyond the walls of this house.

It was not only her identity but also the fact that she was a beautiful young woman, now out and about without escort or chaperone, so leaving herself prey to any of the criminal element that strolled these streets, day as well as night.

'It is not your fault, Evans,' he assured him on a sigh. 'Miss Duprée is...an independent young lady, brought up in the country and used to doing as she wishes. I fear she is not yet used to the ways of the City.'

'I guessed that, Your Grace.' The elderly butler nodded. 'I even offered for her to take young Mary with her for company—the Second Upstairs Maid,' he supplied as Christian looked baffled as to who Mary might be. 'But Miss

Duprée indicated there was no reason to bother or disturb anyone and that she would only take a stroll outside in the fresh air.'

A stroll that had already lasted for two hours or more...

'My cloak and hat, if you please, Evans,' Christian requested wearily. 'If I do not return for another two hours then perhaps you had better send out a search party,' he added drily in parting as he swept out of the front doorway of Sutherland House in search of his errant and rebellious house guest.

# Chapter Twelve

'It is so *bon* to see you, Davy!' Lisette beamed at the young man walking along beside her, aware that he probably did not understand a word she was saying, but hoping to convey her happiness with the brightness of her smile.

She had badly needed to escape Sutherland House earlier, to breathe in the fresh air, to be free for a while of the worry and intrigue that had surrounded her these past few days.

After leaving the house she had taken a stroll about the square outside Sutherland House, as she had given Evans the impression she intended to do. Which had taken her all of ten minutes to complete, and that included pausing to watch a group of small children playing with a ball, watched over by their gossiping nannies.

Having no child of her own to allow to play, and no English either to join in the conversation, Lisette had then ventured out of the square in search of other entertainment.

It had taken some time to reach the shops, and they had proved to be amusing for a while, but as usual she was only window-shopping, having no money to buy any of the pretty lace or fashionable leather gloves on display inside those windows.

It had been shortly after she had given in to the lure of a much bigger park, and become fascinated with watching the ducks swimming happily about on the pond there, that she had spied young Davy, the assistant to the cook on board *The Blue Dolphin*, strolling by.

Fortuitously, because by this time Lisette had walked so far and for so long that she had absolutely no idea how to find her way back to Christian's ducal home.

Conversation between herself and Davy was, as might be expected, a little difficult, but they had managed, between the two of them, to convey the fact that Lisette was well and truly lost in England's capital and Davy had now generously offered to walk back with her to Sutherland House.

Where Lisette would no doubt have to face a wrathful Christian.

She really had not intended to be out for so long or to walk so far, had thought to be back long before Christian rose from his nap. So that perhaps he would not even need to know that she had been out at all.

Instead she had become lost, and no doubt Christian would have been up for some time now and possibly pacing one of those elegantly appointed rooms in Sutherland House as he contemplated what was to be her punishment for having disobeyed him.

In her defence, she had not actually *agreed* with his instruction earlier not to leave Sutherland House.

A poor defence, to be sure, but it was the only one Lisette had in the face of what she knew was going to be Christian's extreme anger for her having disobeyed him.

'Do you have *la famille*—family in London,

Davy?' she prompted curiously as they left the park and began to stroll along the pavement.

'My widowed mother.' He nodded.

Considering that Davy was only aged perhaps sixteen or seventeen, his mother must be a very young widow. 'Any *frères ou soeurs*? Brothers and sisters,' she translated awkwardly.

'Four.' He nodded again. 'Two of each. All younger than me.'

With young Davy no doubt the only bread-winner, Lisette inwardly sympathised, wondering if she dare ask Christian to reward Davy for having returned her safely to Sutherland House.

She already owed Christian so much; what did a little more matter? Besides, she doubted that Christian would wish to make a fuss in front of Davy or Evans.

Once they were alone she had no doubt it would be a different matter...

'How can you have lost her already?' Marcus frowned once Christian had explained the reason for his having called at Worthing House. 'You have only been back in London a few hours!'

A few hours could, when it came to Lisette, as Christian knew only too well, seem as long as a lifetime. Indeed, it seemed like that lifetime since he had left Sutherland House to begin walking the streets in search of her.

His leg ached like the devil, and he had finally given up that search and called upon his sister and brother-in-law at Worthing House, in the tenuous hope that Lisette might have decided to call upon them. An unlikely occurrence, Christian knew, especially as Lisette had no idea where Worthing House even was, but it had now been over three hours since Lisette left to go for a stroll and his anger had been replaced with an uneasy anxiety.

Although he had no doubt that his anger would come boiling back up to the surface the moment he saw her again!

She had the ability, it seemed, to induce strong emotions inside him, be they anger or desire.

'Can you not see how worried he is, my love?' Julianna, glowing with the happiness of her marriage to Worthing and their excitement at their forthcoming baby, now placed a lightly restraining hand upon her husband's arm as the two sat together on the sofa opposite Christian, who sat restlessly on the edge of an armchair. 'Perhaps she has called upon Lord Maystone in the hope of easing that gentleman's mind in regard to her innocence?' she suggested.

It did not surprise Christian in the slightest that Marcus appeared to have told Julianna all. Indeed, he would have been surprised if he had not; the couple had once lost each other because of a lack of communication. Now that they had found each other again and were happily married, they did not intend such misunderstandings to ever happen again.

Christian wished that he could say he had the same open honesty with Lisette.

Although, to be fair, *he* had been the one mainly responsible for having kept secrets.

'Doubtful,' he answered his sister; he could not imagine Lisette voluntarily calling upon Maystone.

'You do believe she is innocent, Christian?' his sister prompted anxiously.

'Without a doubt,' he confirmed distractedly;

he now knew that Lisette was far too headstrong, too outspoken—too forward, he added as he recalled their conversation of earlier—to be in the least proficient at subterfuge. 'She has been gone for *hours*, Marcus.' He gave a shake of his head. 'She is headstrong and impulsive but she is not stupid, and I warned her that it is not safe for her here!'

'Perhaps you should have thought of that before bringing her to England?' Julianna said quietly. 'Although I have to admit to a selfish need to see and speak with her in person, in order that I might thank her for saving my brother's life...'

A sharp reminder from Julianna, perhaps even a rebuke, as to the reason Lisette was in England at all?

Christian sighed heavily. 'I am well aware of what I owe her, Julianna. I just wish—' His mouth firmed. 'She never listens to a word I say to her!'

'Perhaps that is because you do not ask but tell, Christian?'

His jaw tightened at this second rebuke from his sister. 'Asking or telling; neither seems to make the slightest bit of difference. Lisette will always do exactly as she pleases.'

'Another reason why I shall like her!' Julianna's eyes sparkled merrily. 'But I can see how you might find that…irritating.' She sobered as he continued to scowl.

Christian now gave an impatient snort. 'She is stubborn as a mule!'

'She is also missing,' Marcus reminded softly.

'I am well aware of that fact!' Christian stood up to restlessly pace the room, more worried than he cared to admit.

What if Lisette had been set upon by thieves or pickpockets and was even now lying in a gutter somewhere, injured and alone? Or, worse yet, perhaps she had been accosted by those lower-than-low men and women who dealt in the sale of female flesh?

There were any number of scenarios Christian could imagine befalling the naive innocent that Lisette undoubtedly was, albeit a brave one, and each scenario was more horrifying than the last.

'Perhaps you should return to Sutherland House?' Julianna suggested gently. 'Lisette may have returned in your absence and now be worried about you.'

Christian had already thought of that; he had just needed to vent some of his tension, created by his anger and worry over Lisette's whereabouts, before he saw her again. Otherwise he knew he could not be responsible for his actions the moment he set eyes on her again, no matter where they might be or who might be present when it occurred.

'Perhaps you should go with him, my love.' Julianna smiled at Worthing. 'I am sure that Christian would welcome your…moral support at this difficult time.'

'I believe you mean to say my efforts might be required to restrain him from doing poor little Lisette harm when he sees her again.' Worthing gave a boyish grin, obviously enjoying himself, no doubt at Christian's expense.

'Poor little Lisette, my—!' Christian broke off before he was ungentlemanly enough to swear in front of his sister. 'She is also responsible for causing absolute chaos in my life since saving it!' Christian came back disgustedly.

'Well, yes,' Julianna conceded with a slight smile. 'But is that not better than the boredom and ennui that has occasionally bothered you in the past?'

Christian stared at her dumbstruck for a few moments before turning away. 'If you are coming, Worthing, I suggest we leave now.' He did not have an answer to his sister's probing question.

Mainly because he knew Julianna was in the right of it; who could possibly be bored or suffer from ennui when they had the irrepressible Lisette to prevent from becoming embroiled in her next escapade?

Where the *hell* was she?

If she was not back at Sutherland House when he returned, then he would—

He would what?

If Lisette had not returned, three hours after she had supposedly gone for a simple stroll outside in the fresh air, then something must have happened to her. In which case, neither his anger nor his threats to her would be of the slightest significance.

'I am sure she is safe, Christian—'

'You can no more be sure of that than I am, Marcus!' Christian glowered at his brother-in-law a short time later as the two of them travelled back to Sutherland House in Marcus's ducal carriage, a convenience Christian was more grateful for than he cared to admit, his thigh having now become a continuous and painful throb after so much physical exertion.

He somehow knew, as he stepped down from the carriage outside Sutherland House, that Lisette was not contained within its walls. He would have *sensed* her presence there, would have *felt* that quiver of awareness that always seemed to be in the air whenever she was near.

Lisette had not returned.

He knew he was right when a grave-faced Evans opened the door to him and Worthing.

The elderly butler did not even offer to take their hats and cloaks but instead held out a silver tray towards Christian as he entered the hallway. 'This letter was delivered shortly after you left the house, Your Grace.'

'By whom?' Christian prompted sharply.

'A street urchin, it seemed to me.' The butler gave a shake of his head. 'I sent someone to follow him, but they were soon lost in the warren of backstreets. I also sent someone after you, but you could not be found,' he added apologetically as Christian took the letter without comment before ripping it open and quickly reading the contents. 'Is it bad news, Your Grace?' he prompted anxiously.

Christian's hand curled into a fist, crumpling the letter in his palm as he answered reassuringly. 'Nothing for you to worry about, Evans.' He gave a brief if humourless smile. 'Miss Duprée has merely run into an old acquaintance but will be back with us shortly.'

Evans breathed a sigh of relief. 'I am glad to hear it, Your Grace.'

'An old acquaintance…?' Marcus prompted as soon as the two men had retired to the library with a decanter of brandy. 'I did not think Lisette knew anyone in England but us?'

'She does not.' Christian grimly handed the crumpled letter to the other man for him to read. 'It would seem that Lisette has been kidnapped.'

Marcus looked up after quickly reading the letter. 'It is not a very well written letter and the paper is of a quality—'

'Damn the quality of the writing or the paper, Marcus!' Christian exploded angrily. 'They have Lisette, and that is all that is important.'

'Yes, but who are "they"?' Marcus turned the letter over, studying Christian's name and the address written on the front of it. 'Do you think this can be connected with the kidnapping of Maystone's grandson and the abduction of Bea?'

Griffin Stone had almost run Bea down with his carriage after she had escaped her abductors. The two of them were very recently married.

'It is too much of a coincidence for it not to be,' Christian bit out grimly as he recalled that young lady's harsh treatment during her incarceration. The thought of Lisette being treated harshly was enough to turn the blood cold in Christian's veins.

'But we already have those responsible in custody—'

'Not all of them.' Christian's hand shook as he raised the glass of brandy to his lips and took a much-needed swallow of the fiery liquid before speaking again. 'We—*I* did not apprehend Helene Rousseau.'

'You were not sent to Paris to apprehend her—' Marcus broke off, eyes widening. 'Do you believe that she is capable of arranging something so abhorrent as the abduction of her own daughter…?'

Christian recalled the pistol that had been pressed against his spine that very first evening at the Fleur de Lis, when Helene Rousseau had thought he was paying far too much attention to Lisette. She had seemed like a hen protecting her chick that night—albeit a steely-cold one!—and yet it really was too much of a coincidence to believe there could be two sets of kidnappers in so short a time. Helene Rousseau *had* to be involved in Lisette's disappearance.

The alternative was too disturbing to contemplate.

Christian's jaw tightened. 'It clearly says in the letter that Maystone is to be at Westminster Bridge at midnight tonight if we want to see Lisette again. Why else would they involve

Maystone if this was not connected to the kidnapping of his grandson and the abduction of Griffin's Bea?'

Why else indeed...?

How could she have been so stupid, so *naive*, Lisette admonished herself as she looked about the windowless room in which she was being held a prisoner, a dirty handkerchief secured about her mouth, her wrists and ankles bound with thin but strong cord; she knew it was strong because all of her efforts to free herself had proved to be in vain.

As if Davy would really have just been strolling in a London park, when the last time she had seen him had been at the Portsmouth dock as she and Christian departed *The Blue Dolphin*. She should have guessed—*known*—the moment she saw Davy again that it was too much of a coincidence for him to now be in London.

Instead, she had been so pleased to see a familiar face, after realising she was lost, that she had not questioned *why* she was seeing that face.

Lisette had assumed, even as Davy directed her through an unsavoury area of London that she did not remember walking through earlier, that he knew the capital so well that he was taking a shortcut back to Sutherland House. Instead, another man had suddenly emerged from a dark alley, throwing a sack over her head while Davy bound her wrists, and she was then bundled into a smelly cart and taken to the house in which this windowless room was situated.

The sack had not been removed from her head until she had stumbled into the room, Davy remaining in the background as the other man, hat pulled low over his eyes, a kerchief about the lower half of his face, had secured the gag and then bound her hands and feet, before they both departed, Lisette assumed, to another part of this hovel.

She had no idea if Davy was acting alone with his accomplice, in an effort to extract money for her release, or if her abduction had a much deeper significance.

Whichever of those it was, Lisette knew that Christian would be very displeased with her when he learned what had happened; he had tried to warn her of the dangers of leaving the house alone. She, with her usual stubbornness, had thought she knew better and had refused to believe there could possibly be anyone in England who might want to harm her.

Her reward for that naivety was to be held prisoner in this dark room, gagged and bound.

With the added worry that, as she was nothing more than a rebellious nuisance to Christian, he may not feel inclined to pay a ransom for her release even if one should be demanded.

The situation was dire enough to make her sit and cry. If self-pity had been in her nature. And if she thought it would have done any good.

It was not, and she knew crying would only make her feel more miserable when her mouth was gagged and her hands tied.

No, she had no choice but to remain in this unpleasant place until such time as she was either released or—

Lisette did not wish to contemplate what that *or* might be.

'Well, of course I will go to Westminster Bridge and meet with these people tonight, Christian,'

Maystone assured him testily as Christian scowled down at him as he sat in a chair in his own drawing room. 'It is not a question of whether I go or not.'

'Then what is it a question of?' Christian was too restless to be seated himself, preferring to pace the room instead.

The older man sighed heavily, his face pale. 'What might be demanded of me in exchange for Miss Duprée's release.'

Christian was well aware of the demons of hell Maystone had suffered for weeks, when his loyalty to the Crown prevented him from yielding the information demanded of him in exchange for his grandson's safe return.

The same demons of hell Christian had been suffering since he had received word of Lisette's abduction. Which, in actual time, had only been a matter of just over an hour.

It seemed much longer.

As he knew the five hours until midnight would seem interminable.

Christian's mouth thinned. 'Whatever it is they want, you will give it to them.'

The older man looked up at him regretfully. 'You know I cannot do that, Christian.'

Yes, he did know that; if Maystone had been unwilling to give in to blackmail in exchange for his grandson's life, then he was unlikely to do so for a young woman he had only met for the first time earlier today. A young woman, moreover, who was known to be the illegitimate daughter of the same woman who had organised the kidnapping of Maystone's grandson.

'I think we may both safely assume that this unpleasant business does at least confirm Lisette to be innocent of all wrongdoing,' Maystone proffered gently. 'Unless, of course, she was aware of this plan all along and is in cahoots with her supposed abductors…?'

The idea had also occurred—very briefly—to Christian and been just as quickly dismissed. Lisette had been brought to London against her will or intention. And the Lisette who had offered to become his mistress earlier today simply did not have it in her to behave in so underhand a manner.

She was infuriating, rebellious to the point of endangering her own safety, but he believed beyond a shadow of a doubt that Lisette was not, and never could be, a liar.

He glared at Maystone. 'You *will* give these people whatever they demand for her safe return,' he growled.

Maystone surged impatiently to his feet at Christian's accusing tone. 'You know of my limitations in that regard as well as I, Christian.'

'Damn it to hell—!' Christian wanted to put his fist through something in order to vent his frustration and anger.

Every minute that passed was one more minute he could not be sure if Lisette still lived; she would not be the first kidnap victim to have been disposed of shortly after being taken, the kidnappers' only interest in the ransom. His only consolation was that Maystone's grandson had been found unharmed, if badly shaken.

But even that was of little comfort. Worthing had a point earlier; the people who had Lisette could not be the same ones who had taken the boy because they were currently incarcerated in prison, awaiting trial.

'I understand how you are feeling, Christian,' Maystone consoled him.

Christian was not sure how he was 'feeling', so he very much doubted that the other man could possibly know or understand either.

On the one hand, Christian felt almost paralysed with worry as to Lisette's safety.

On the other, he wanted to *do* something—something tangible towards facilitating her return.

He was also furious with Lisette for her recklessness, at the same time as he needed to hold her in his arms and reassure himself that she was safe and unharmed.

So many mixed emotions, all running around inside him, with Lisette at the heart of all of them.

*The heart...*

Christian was an educated man, and that intellect told him that emotions came from a person's head and not their heart, as the romantics liked to wax lyrical.

But if that was so, then why had his chest *ached* so much since he learned of Lisette's abduction? As if a heavy weight had been placed upon it, restricting his breathing and making him feel nauseous.

'She will not allow her to be harmed, Christian.'

'She?' He looked sharply at Maystone.

The older man sighed. 'Helene Rousseau.'

'We cannot be sure she is behind this.'

'I am.' Aubrey Maystone moved to replenish his brandy glass, holding the decanter up questioningly to Christian and replacing it back on the tray when he gave an impatiently dismissive shake of his head.

'How so?' Christian finally prompted irritably when he could stand the other man's silence no longer.

Maystone looked at him with calm blue eyes. 'Because I believe I now know the reason that I, and *my* grandson in particular, was made the target two months ago.'

'Which is?'

The other man closed his eyes briefly before

opening them again to reveal a look of stoic resolve. 'I was not always the elderly man you now see before you, Christian. I was once a young man very like you and the other Dangerous Dukes.' He gave a self-derisive twist of his lips in the semblance of a smile. 'I too wanted to set right the wrongs in the world, craved adventure, intrigue—'

'I do not see—'

'—was impatient with the caution of others,' Maystone continued pointedly. 'Believed that action was what was needed, not talk and political compromise.'

Christian's hands were clenched into fists at his sides. 'If there is a point to this conversation, Aubrey, then I wish you would get to it!'

The older man sighed. 'There is a point, but it is not one I can share with you just yet. Suffice to say,' he continued when Christian would have interrupted, 'if I am still alive when this is all finally over, I shall be resigning my post.'

'If you are still alive...?'

'Have you not accepted yet that *I* have been

the target all along?' He gave a rueful shake of his head. 'A very personal, very definite target.'

'Why should you think that?' He stared at the other man incredulously.

'I have been compromised, Christian, and in a way I could never have expected.' He gave another deep sigh before brightening. 'But we will get your Lisette back to you—'

'She is not my Lisette—'

'No?' Maystone raised iron-grey brows. 'Well, never mind that for now,' he continued briskly. 'For the moment you and I are going to eat dinner together—'

'I cannot eat whilst Lisette is no doubt alone and frightened as to what will happen to her!'

'We will eat dinner together,' Maystone repeated firmly. 'Discuss the weather, and all those other boring subjects that are considered correct conversation in polite society, and then at midnight we will go to Westminster Bridge and retrieve Lisette. Trust me, Christian.' The other man placed a reassuring hand on his arm. 'No harm will come to her.'

Somehow the other man's words of reassurance had the opposite effect on Christian; he was now more worried than ever that before the night was out someone was going to die.

# Chapter Thirteen

Lisette knew that in her present circumstances she should not be admiring the beauty of her surroundings as she stood on the bridge between her two abductors. One of which she knew to be Davy, the other remaining silent and hidden beneath that cloak, kerchief and the hat pulled low over his eyes.

She should not be appreciating her surroundings, but it was impossible for her not to be grateful for the fresh air she was breathing into her lungs after the stale air in that closed room. Or to be affected by the atmosphere of the night, with the gentle glow of the street lamps overhead casting shadows on the softly flowing river below.

Of course, she would have been happier if

she was not still gagged and had her wrists tied behind her back, but Davy's one attempt to re-move the gag had resulted in her screaming so loudly he had proclaimed she had 'fair deaf-ened' him with the noise, before he had hastily replaced it.

A nasty smelly piece of now damp rag, which literally made her want to gag every time the smell assailed her nose.

Still, she was at least out of that dark room, and with only these two men to guard her she had hoped for the possibility of escape.

Except there had been no opportunity to do so as she was pushed back into that uncomfortable cart before being brought here to this bridge, the two men now seeming to be waiting for some-thing. Or someone.

Christian?

Lisette could not think of anyone else who would be in the least interested in whether she lived or died. After her earlier disobedience of his instruction, she was not altogether sure that Christian would be interested either.

But she could hope.

\* \* \*

Christian could see the three figures standing beneath a guttering street lamp at the far end of the bridge as he and Maystone alighted from his carriage together. None of them looked to be very big, but he was sure that the slighter one in the middle was Lisette. He hoped and prayed the middle one was Lisette, as much as he hoped and prayed that she was unharmed.

'The note said I must go alone, Christian,' Maystone reminded as he placed his hat determinedly upon his head.

'They may be armed—'

'I too am armed,' he reminded quietly, having hidden a pistol in the waistband at the back of his pantaloons. Not the most convenient of places for him to retrieve it, but it would not do to reveal he was armed from the onset. 'But I doubt it will be necessary,' he added softly, his gaze fixed on the three figures on the bridge.

Christian was also armed with a pistol, but he knew that he would never be able to make his shot anything near accurate from this distance.

'What are you not telling me, Aubrey?' He eyed the other man frustratedly.

Maystone gave him a calm smile. 'Does your Lisette possess a temper, Christian?'

'She is not— Yes,' he confirmed impatiently as Maystone raised mocking brows. 'Lisette has a very fine temper indeed.'

'I believed that might be the case.' Maystone nodded. 'A word of advice, Christian: whatever you do, never be the one to incite that temper.'

'Oh, I believe it is far too late for that!' he murmured drily as he recalled the names Lisette had called him in her tirade both yesterday and again today.

'I have no doubt you are more than up to the challenge.' Maystone chuckled as he held out his hand. 'I am glad to have known you, Christian.'

He slowly reached out to take that hand and return the handshake.

'You are a man any parent would be proud to call his son.' The older man nodded in satisfaction.

'What—?'

'Never fear; I will send Lisette back to you

in just a few minutes.' He straightened. 'You will find several letters on my desk at home; if I could ask that you deliver them to the appropriate people if I should not return?'

Christian was liking the sound of this less and less.

'Strangest thing about women,' Maystone mused as he stared across the bridge. 'Softest creatures on earth when they are loved, and the most vicious when they are not.'

'Aubrey—'

'I am not rambling, I assure you, Christian,' he continued briskly. 'Wait here for Lisette.'

'But—'

'You will do as I ask, Christian.' The older man's eyes glowed with determination.

Leaving Christian with no choice but to stand and watch as Aubrey Maystone began to walk across the bridge to where Lisette and her abductors waited.

Of one thing Lisette was certain; the man walking across the bridge towards them was not Christian. This man was not tall or broad enough in the shoulders to be him.

And yet he seemed to be walking purposefully towards them. Just as Lisette could also sense the increased tension in the man beside her, the one whose face was covered by the kerchief. As if he knew and recognised the man, if Lisette did not.

Except she did, of course; once the man passed beneath one of the flickering lamps, she was able to make out that he was none other than Lord Aubrey Maystone.

A man who had no reason to trust her, and surely had absolutely no interest in saving her.

'Is that really necessary?' He stopped just feet away to indicate the gag about Lisette's mouth and the rope about her wrists.

'She's a screamer,' Davy muttered.

Lord Maystone pinned him with his steely blue gaze. 'You would no doubt scream too, young man, if you had been abducted and held a prisoner these past six hours or more! Remove the gag and ropes immediately,' he instructed authoritatively.

Davy turned to look at his accomplice, as if for direction. A direction he received as the other man gave a dismissive wave of his gloved hand without once looking away from Lord Maystone.

Lisette drew in a grateful breath the moment the gag was removed from her mouth; even the pungent odour of the river was more pleasant than the smelly rag.

She was even more relieved when the cord had been removed from about her wrists. Allowing her to rub the numbed flesh and let the blood flow freely to her fingers as she stepped tentatively away from her abductors, moving more quickly as they made no attempt to stop her.

'You are unharmed, my dear?' Lord Maystone prompted gruffly as she reached his side.

'No thanks to these two men,' she confirmed with a narrow-eyed and accusing glare at Davy, who at least had the grace to shift uncomfortably.

The elderly man nodded. 'In that case, you may return to Christian while I— You will let her go to him, Helene,' he rasped harshly as the man with the kerchief stepped forward as if to prevent Lisette from leaving.

*Helene...?*

Lisette turned to look wonderingly at the man—woman?—wearing the kerchief, just in time to see that kerchief pulled down and to find herself looking into the hard uncompromising face of the woman who claimed to be her mother.

She felt the blood leach from her cheeks at the realisation that her own mother had been one of her abductors. 'I do not understand...'

Lord Maystone gave a regretful smile. 'I have only just begun to do so—' He broke off as he quickly reached forward to drag Lisette behind him as Helene Rousseau drew a pistol from the waistband of the rough trousers she was wearing.

'I said you were to come alone,' Helene rasped in accented English, her pistol pointed not at Maystone or Lisette but at someone behind them.

Lisette turned to see that Christian now stood just a few feet away, his own pistol aimed at Helene's heart; his approach had been made so stealthily that none on the bridge, least of all Lisette, seemed to have been aware of him standing there until Helene was finally alerted to his presence.

Lisette gave a wince as she saw the dangerous coldness of Christian's expression as he continued to aim his pistol at Helene. A cold intensity of purpose that prevented Lisette from gauging his mood towards her.

Although she knew that it could not be in the least favourable, when she had put not only herself in danger with her impetuousness, but now also Lord Maystone and Christian himself.

She had every intention of apologising to him for her reckless stupidity if—*when* they had all escaped from this situation unharmed.

In the meantime, she was still finding it difficult to believe that Helene was in London at all, let alone that she had been instrumental in her abduction. The other woman must have followed on another ship almost immediately after their own sloop had left France.

'Put the pistol down, Helene,' Lord Maystone was the one to instruct firmly. 'Before someone gets hurt. Undoubtedly yourself, considering that Christian is an expert shot and unlikely to miss from such close proximity.'

Helene's nostrils flared. 'It is a pity my men did not succeed in disposing of him five days ago.'

Maystone chuckled ruefully as Lisette gave an indignant gasp. 'It is as well for you that they did not, otherwise I fear we would not be having this conversation at all.'

Helene's eyes glittered malevolently as she now turned her pistol onto him. 'I did not come here to talk.'

'I am well aware of it, my dear,' Lord Maystone accepted wearily. 'And I am completely at your service, if you could first allow Lisette and Christian to depart, and perhaps this young man?' He indicated Davy, now standing back in the shadows.

'I have no intention of going anywhere,' Christian stated firmly, completely baffled as to Helene Rousseau's presence in London, but totally aware that it boded ill for any who were acquainted with her cold ruthlessness.

'Nor I,' Lisette stated just as determinedly.

*That* was not his intention, Christian acknowledged with frustration. Although, knowing Lisette's stubbornness, he should have expected it. 'Were it not for your rebelliousness of nature, then none of us would be here at all,' he reminded harshly.

A guilty blush instantly coloured her cheeks, her lashes becoming downcast, but for once she remained silent.

Christian found that he disliked Lisette's silence even more than he had enjoyed her outspokenness in regard to himself these past few days.

As much as he disliked the fact that she remained at Maystone's side once she achieved her release. Perhaps understandably when his own anger must be so apparent. Lisette obviously did not realise it, but it was an anger born of anxiety, rather than anything else.

'As the young people both seem bent on being a part of this conversation—' Aubrey Maystone spoke lightly '—perhaps we might all, with the exception of your young accomplice, retire to the comfort of Sutherland's carriage for the rest of it? Away from prying eyes and listening ears.'

Helene Rousseau gave him a contemptuous glance. 'I have nothing to say to you.'

'Nothing?' He quirked steely brows.

Her mouth thinned. 'No.'

'Just want the satisfaction of putting a bullet through my heart, hmm?' the older man said drily.

The Frenchwoman gave a hard feral smile. 'I have thought of little else for some time now.'

Christian could see the bewilderment in Lisette's expression and knew that it must reflect his own. Maystone had never mentioned knowing Helene Rousseau personally during all these months they had been investigating her and her brother, and yet it was obvious from the conversation that the two had met before.

An uneasy feeling had begun to settle in the depths of Christian's chest.

'Dear, dear, Helene,' Maystone chided mockingly. 'Has no one ever told you that vengeance invariably destroys the avenger rather than the victim of that vengeance?'

She eyed him contemptuously. 'And yet I am the one standing here with a pistol aimed at your treacherous heart.'

'Oh, I did not for a moment mean that you would not kill me, my dear—' Maystone spoke calmly of his own imminent murder in cold blood '—only that by doing so you stand a chance of losing the one thing that matters to you. Am I right?'

Christian was now standing close enough that he could see Helene Rousseau's eyes narrow in warning. 'Perhaps it *would* be best if we were all to retire to my carriage,' he suggested mildly, his pistol remaining unwavering on the French-woman as he turned to look at the boy linger-ing in the shadows. 'You and I will talk again, young Davy,' he added.

'She made me do it!' He stepped forward in alarm. 'I only went to the tavern for a drink or two that last night ashore in Paris, and—and— She plied me with free liquor and threatened to 'ave someone 'arm me mam if I didn't do as she asked!'

'Which was?'

'To leave word for her at Portsmouth as to where you and the young lady 'ad gone—er—Your Grace. To follow you and then wait for her arrival. I couldn't let nuffink 'appen to me mam, Your Grace,' he added desperately. 'She's all me brothers and sisters 'ave while I'm away at sea. I mean, I like the young lady well enough, but—'

'You are excused, Davy,' Christian interrupted wearily, having no wish to hear how much Davy 'liked' Lisette. He was also well aware of the methods of persuasion of which Helene Rousseau was capable. 'But a lesson has been well learned, I hope?'

'Your Grace?' Davy wrinkled his grubby brow in concentration.

Christian grimaced his exasperation. 'In future, stay away from French taverns and free liquor.'

'Oh.' The grubby brow cleared. 'I will, Your Grace. Thank you, Your Grace.' He touched a greasy forelock.

'Just go, Davy.' Christian sighed, waiting until the young lad had scuttled away into the darkness before turning back to the woman who had put the fear of God into the boy. 'I trust he, and his family, need not live in fear of any retribution from you?'

Helene Rousseau gave a dismissive snort. 'He was merely a means to an end and is of as much importance to me as the flea on a dog!'

Christian nodded his satisfaction with her answer. 'Then if we might all adjourn to my carriage...?'

Lisette had to admit to being baffled by all that had happened these past few hours—these past few minutes especially.

Helene in London.

The fact that she and Lord Maystone obviously knew each other.

That Helene stated she now wished to kill him.

It seemed to Lisette that everything that had happened these past few months—the kidnapping of Lord Maystone's grandson, Helene's anger at Lisette's...friendship with Christian— a friendship Lisette had almost certainly put in jeopardy with her reckless behaviour—her own abduction earlier today—had all been leading to

this face-to-face meeting between Helene Rousseau and Lord Maystone.

Because of some past wrong Helene believed
he had done to her.

The shooting of Helene's brother André, perhaps?

Not personally, of course; Lisette had learned
from one of the other serving girls at the tavern
that her uncle André had been gunned down outside the tavern in a street brawl. But perhaps a
brawl that had been arranged by Lord Maystone?

*That* did not make any sense when André
Rousseau had met his end only months ago,
and Helene's grudge against Lord Maystone appeared to be one of long standing.

And if it was of such long standing, why had
Helene not sought vengeance before now?

What had happened in Helene's life in the past
few months to bring about this sudden need for
vengeance—?

Lisette stilled, eyes widening as she turned
to look at the woman who had come to the Duprées' farm and claimed to be her mother less
than three months ago.

The advent into Helene's life of Lisette, her illegitimate daughter, was what had changed for Helene Rousseau in these past months.

*She* was the reason Helene was here seeking vengeance against Lord Maystone.

If that was true, then Lisette could think of only ohe reason for it being so.

'If you will excuse my sudden movement, Helene?' Lord Maystone remarked conversationally as he stepped forward. 'But I do believe our daughter is about to faint.' He gathered Lisette into his arms as she began to sink gracefully to the ground.

## Chapter Fourteen

'You should have told me you were with child.'

'*You* had made it clear to me that you were returning to England to your wife and family!'

'Which I duly did. But that still did not prevent you from informing me that you were expecting my child. I could have made provision for you—and her—'

'I did not want your charity—'

'And what about her? Did she not deserve better?'

'I did the best for her that I could, ensured she was placed with a loving couple—'

'Would the two of you please be silent?' Christian cut icily through the argument that had been going on for some time now. Without any pistols in evidence, thank goodness; he could not be answerable for not placing a bullet in both Maystone and Helene Rousseau himself if he had to listen to too much more of their to-and-fro bickering.

And all the time the object of their argument lay recumbent upon the chaise in Christian's drawing room, covered with the blanket he had demanded from Evans as he carried Lisette into the house, and still unconscious from her faint at Westminster Bridge.

Christian had wasted no time in putting his pistol away and relieving Maystone of the burden of Lisette, ushering her back across the bridge towards his carriage, uncaring whether Maystone and the woman who was his ex-lover followed him or not. His only concern had been for Lisette.

It still was.

She had remained unconscious for the whole of the carriage ride back to Sutherland House, no doubt from fatigue and the relief of knowing she was free as much as anything else. Even Lisette, with her indomitable will, must have been traumatised by her abduction and imprisonment goodness knew where.

Having subsequently realised, as he was sure she had, that Lord Aubrey Maystone was her father must have been the final straw that had broken that indomitable will.

Christian had to admit to being more than a little surprised at that disclosure himself. How on earth had Lord Aubrey Maystone, a man who worked in the shadows for the government and Crown, even met a woman like Helene Rousseau, let alone—let alone— The idea of the two of them having engaged in an affair twenty years ago was astounding—

'I did try to explain earlier that I was once very like you, Christian.' Maystone gently interrupted his thoughts. 'Twenty-five years ago I was also an agent for the Crown, as you are now. My duties often took me to France, and it was during one of these…forays twenty years ago, for information, that I chanced to meet Helene.'

Christian grimaced. 'It would seem that you did more than "meet" her!'

'Yes. Well.' The older man looked uncomfortable. 'I have never claimed to be a saint.'

'Neither have I—but I do not believe I have ever impregnated a woman and then abandoned her!'

The older man closed his eyes briefly. 'It was not like that.'

'Then pray tell us what it was "like"?' Lisette finally stirred from lying prone on the chaise, her head aching as she sat up. She felt unable to even glance at Christian as he stood beside the window, for fear of the condemnation she might see in his face that her actions earlier had brought them all to this. Instead she chose to look only at the man and woman she now knew to be her parents.

A more unlikely couple she could not imagine—Helene so tall and fierce, Aubrey Maystone several inches shorter, and with an aristocratic face that now softened into lines of concern as he looked across at her.

*Her father.*

Lord Aubrey Maystone was her father.

The very *English* Lord Aubrey Maystone.

Lisette had been in turmoil as to who her father might be since learning that Helene was her mother; it did not seem possible, after the fears Lisette had harboured in regard to this English Lord for the past few days, to now learn that he was also the man who had fathered her.

He stood up now, as if he might come to her, but instead he began pacing in front of the fireplace when Lisette glared at him almost as fiercely as Helene was now doing. 'Once I learned earlier today that you were Helene's daughter—' He gave a shake of his head. 'I knew the moment I saw you that you must also be my own daughter.' He looked at Lisette wonderingly. 'You look exactly like my sister—your aunt Anna,' he explained at her wide-eyed look.

Lisette recalled the way he had stared at her when they were introduced earlier. 'I have an aunt…?'

He nodded. 'And several half-brothers and sisters, and nieces and nephews—'

'Let us not become distracted with a list of Lisette's English relatives.' Christian stepped forward into the centre of the room. 'Surely you all must see that this situation is… It is far more complicated than I could ever have imagined.' Although he did have some explanation, at least, as to why Maystone had seemed so befuddled earlier today when he met Lisette for the first time.

And it had also not escaped Christian's notice that Lisette had not so much as glanced in his direction since she regained consciousness.

Because she felt awkward, having now learned of her true parentage?

Perhaps because she now felt uncomfortable recalling their own conversation earlier today, when she had offered to become his mistress?

Or it might just be that she was aware this present situation had come about because she had disobeyed him, and so allowed for her own abduction?

The former she was most certainly not responsible for.

Nor could Christian ever have contemplated taking Lisette as his mistress.

And he was no longer sure Lisette could be

held even partly responsible for her own abduction either.

For one thing, Helene Rousseau had obviously been bent on reclaiming her daughter, as well as seeking vengeance on her erstwhile lover. Christian was now convinced that if the older woman had not abducted Lisette when she had, she would only have found another day when she might do so.

As for Lisette disobeying him… Christian had *known* she was upset earlier, after he had rejected her offer to become his mistress.

Just as he had known how headstrong she was.

Consequently he should have had more safeguards put in place to prevent her from straying outside the house. At the very least, he should have alerted Evans to the fact that Lisette might attempt to do exactly that, and to wake him immediately if it should occur. Instead, several hours had elapsed—including his lazing in the bath for almost an hour—before he was even made aware Lisette had left the house.

If anyone or anything was to blame for what she had suffered today, then it was Christian's own arrogance in having believed he could issue a mandate to Lisette and expect her to obey it without question.

She had felt so tiny in his arms earlier, so fragile as he carried her across the bridge. A painful reminder of how close he had come to losing her.

Just the thought of that was indeed painful.

He had, he realised, become accustomed to having Lisette in his life—arguing with her, teasing her, laughing with her, *making love to her*. Even after only a few hours of her presence, his house had seemed empty without her in it.

His *life* would be equally empty without her in it.

But if she really was Maystone's daughter— and the other man appeared to have no doubts on the matter—then Christian knew he had already lost the Lisette he knew. Not to kidnappers, or death, as he had feared earlier, but to the father who would surely now claim her as his own.

There would be a brief scandal, of course—Lisette had been born during Maystone's marriage, after all—but she was not the first illegitimate child to have later been given legitimacy when claimed by her father. Maystone was certainly more than powerful enough to weather such a storm.

And Lisette?

Lisette had already ably demonstrated her own fortitude.

She would possibly object initially, but with time she would no doubt become the polished, the Honourable Miss Lisette Maystone.

And while she might politely acknowledge Christian Seaton, the Duke of Sutherland, at a ball or some other society entertainment, they would meet as polite strangers, would no longer be the Lisette and Christian they had been for these past days.

*Arguing. Teasing. Laughing. Making love together.*

That realisation was enough to bring back the heavy ache in his chest.

'I do not see any complication; Lisette is my daughter, and I will immediately acknowledge her as such,' Maystone announced predictably. 'Unless, of course, you are still intent on shooting me?' He glanced ruefully at Helene Rousseau.

'Do not mock me, *monsieur*!' Helene glared at him.

'I am not mocking you.' He sighed wearily. 'I am only sorry that my actions twenty years ago have caused such a deep and abiding resentment inside you. You were responsible for the kidnapping of my grandson two months ago, were you not?'

Her face flushed. 'For Napoleon's cause—'

'Not for Napoleon's cause, Helene, but your own,' Maystone corrected softly. 'You no doubt thought to pay me back in some measure for what you considered my cavalier treatment of you all those years ago. You should not have used an innocent child as a weapon, Helene,' he rebuked her. 'I am perfectly willing to pay for my crimes, but Michael and his parents did not deserve to suffer in that way.'

'And what of my innocent child?' Helene challenged.

'If you had told me all those years ago, come to me after Lisette was born even, then Lisette need not have suffered either!'

'You would not have acknowledged her as your

daughter while your wife still lived,' the French-woman said scornfully.

'I would have ensured that she wanted for nothing—'

'You would not have acknowledged her!'

'I will acknowledge her now. And gladly,' Maystone assured her fervently. '*If* you should choose not to shoot me, Lisette will stay here in England with me, as my recognised daughter.'

'And if I do not agree?'

'I will of course listen to your arguments regarding the pros and cons of the situation—'

'And then do just as you wish, as you always have!'

'Am I to have no say in this matter?' Lisette now rose impatiently to her feet, having heard enough from both these people who claimed to be her parents. 'I am not a sweetmeat for the two of you to fight over. I am a person. With—with feelings of my own.' Tears stung her eyes. 'Three months ago I lived on a farm and believed the Duprées were my parents. I then learned that I was the illegitimate daughter of tavern owner Helene Rousseau. Now I am expected to accept that I am also the daughter of an English lord.' She threw her hands up in disgust. 'What if I should decide I do not wish to live with either of you? If—if I wish to establish my own household? Separate from either of you?'

Lord Maystone—her father—looked disconcerted. 'It really is not the done thing for a single young lady to establish her own household—'

'For an English young lady, perhaps,' Lisette accepted stubbornly. 'But I am not English.'

'You could be, and in just a little time.' Lord Maystone nodded. 'I will hire a tutor to teach you to speak the language, and my daughter-in-law will, I am sure, give her advice on the correct gowns. In no time at all you will be an English young lady, and it will very soon be forgotten that you were ever French—'

'Not by me!' Lisette insisted exasperatedly. 'I *am* French. I am proud to be French. And I will not deny my birthplace to suit English *société*.'

'But my dear—'

'Do not "my dear" me!' Lisette all but stamped her foot in her increasing frustration with this situation. 'A very short time ago I believed you would put me in chains and lock me away, simply because I am Helene Rousseau's daughter—'

'Are you responsible for telling her such a thing, Christian?' Maystone frowned at him.

'He did not need to do so,' Lisette continued impatiently. 'It was to be expected, when I am the daughter of a known conspirator against your English Crown. Except now I am expected to believe that you will not lock me in chains after all, because you are *mon père*.' She gave a shake of her head. 'I cannot so easily adjust to all these sudden changes in my life.'

'Nor should you be expected to do so.' Christian decided it was time—past time—that he intervened on Lisette's behalf. 'Madame Rousseau, Lord Maystone, I suggest for the moment that Lisette remains here at Sutherland House with me. That she be given time in which to… to come to terms with these sudden changes in her circumstances so that she might then make an educated judgement as to which life suits her best, England or France.'

'Impossible!'

*'Impossible!'*

At last the older couple seemed to agree on something. Even if it was Christian's suggestion that Lisette should remain here with him.

It was an impossible solution; he had known that before making it. Wanting something did not make it so.

Just as he knew his reasons for making it were totally selfish ones.

He simply could not bear the thought of losing Lisette, of the two of them becoming polite strangers to each other.

'Madame Rousseau.' He turned to look at her between narrowed lids. 'You knew Lisette had come to my home that night in Paris, so why did you not do more to prevent her from travelling to England with me?'

'I followed on the next available ship—'

'Why did you wait at all, when the two of you had argued— I do not appreciate the fact that you struck Lisette, by the way,' he added darkly.

'It was a mistake—an impulse— She is so headstrong, I could not make her see reason,' Helene admitted heavily. 'I deeply regret ever striking you, Lisette. I only wanted to save you from…from making a fool of yourself, as I did over your father.' She shot Maystone a scathing glance.

Christian did not wish to begin *that* particular argument all over again. 'That still does not explain why you allowed Lisette to come to England with me and then followed her.'

Helene's chin rose. 'I came here to take her back with me, of course.'

'Why?'

*'Pourquoi?'* she repeated. 'I do not understand…'

Christian sighed. 'You do not even acknowledge Lisette as being your daughter, so why would you even bother following her and trying to take her back to Paris with you? Why did you abduct her? In order to bring Maystone to you? So that you might kill him?' Christian continued determinedly. 'Or was it for another reason entirely?'

Helene's eyes narrowed on Maystone. 'He deserves to die. He made love to me then returned to his wife without giving me a second thought, and left me with child!'

Christian's mouth twisted wryly as he glanced at Lisette. 'You really are your mother's daughter.'

Lisette felt the colour heat her cheeks at the memory of the insults she'd thrown at Christian just yesterday.

It seemed so much longer than just a single day had passed since she verbally vented her anger at Christian at the inn in Portsmouth.

So much had happened in the past thirty-six hours that she really did feel at a loss to comprehend it, to take it all in, let alone make a life-changing decision.

Quite what Christian made of it all she did not like to hazard a guess.

He now gave a shake of his head. 'There must have been any number of opportunities for you to…dispose of Maystone these past twenty years, *madame*. Why should you feel such a need to make him suffer now? To exact your revenge? To think of killing him? Or was it for another reason entirely that you wished to introduce Lord Maystone to his daughter?'

'I do not— He is not— Bah!' Helene threw up her hands in disgust.

Christian gave a rueful grimace. 'Can it be that, in your own way, you do love your daughter? That you wish only the best for her? Even if you have now realised that best is not with you in a tavern in Paris?'

Lisette looked sharply at the woman who had given birth to her; she still could not think of her as her mother. Helene continued to look at Christian, eyes glittering.

'I remember the night we all met at your tavern in Paris, *madame*,' Christian continued softly. 'Your threat to shoot me—a habit you really should think of breaking!—if I should even think of laying so much as a hand upon Lisette.'

Colour darkened Helene's cheeks. 'You— I— You are an English spy!'

'At that moment I was only a man looking at your daughter with lustful eyes.' He shrugged as Lisette gave a shocked gasp. 'I'm first and foremost a man, Lisette,' he excused drily. 'And that night you stood out as pure as a rose amongst lesser, bruised blooms.'

'Helene…?' Maystone prompted softly.

'I do not— I am—' She broke off, her mouth thinning stubbornly.

'I believe, despite everything, Madame Rousseau, that you are a mother who wants what is best for her daughter,' Christian continued softly. 'You were young when she was born, and no doubt it seemed the best thing for all if she was placed with foster parents. But, from the little Lisette has told me, you went immediately to claim her the moment you realised those foster parents had both died. That is not the behaviour of a woman who did not care for her child.'

Lisette had never thought of Helene's actions in quite that way before…

She saw now that Christian was right.

She had no knowledge of Helene until that day she came to the farm for her, no awareness that the Duprées were not her real parents. Helene could so easily have ignored Lisette's existence, and merely thought herself fortunate in no longer having the burden of paying for her child's upkeep.

Instead Helene had taken her to live with her in

Paris. Not an ideal situation, for either of them, but she could see now that Helene had perhaps done her best in the circumstances.

'You love me…?' she prompted tentatively.

Helene looked first irritated and then exasperated. 'Of course I love you, you stupid child! Perhaps I do not have the necessary skills to be *votre mère*, but I tried as best I could to protect you. *You* were the one who constantly threw yourself in the path of danger, first with Le Duc and now here again in London.'

'A habit I have also tried—and failed—to curb, *madame*,' Christian drawled.

Lisette gave him a quelling glance before turning back to Helene. 'You believed that following me to England, arranging for me to be kidnapped and then threatening to kill *mon père* in front of my eyes, having just discovered who he was, to be an effective way of protecting me?'

'She would never have shot him, Lisette,' Christian chided gently. 'That was not your intention at all, was it, *madame*?'

'He—'

'I am not interested in what he did or did not

do twenty years ago.' Christian spoke firmly. 'It is here and now that is important.'

Helene seemed to fight a battle within herself for some seconds before her shoulders slumped. 'I have tried, these past months, to be a mother to Lisette, but I simply do not— The tavern is not—' She gave a shake of her head. 'She is not happy there, and I am not happy for her to be there either. Not for the reason you suppose, Lisette,' she added softly as she flinched. 'You do not belong in such a place; I knew that from the start. I became convinced of it when the Comte took such an interest in you.'

Lisette frowned. 'If that is true, why did you not simply contact *mon père* and ask him to take me, rather than go through this elaborate charade to achieve your aim?'

'Pride,' Lord Maystone put in gently. 'I believe, my dear Lisette, that when judging your mother you should also consider my own part in all of this. As far as Helene was concerned, I had abandoned her. She is a proud woman. A strong and independent woman. To have asked me for help now would have been—' He looked at Helene. 'It simply could not have been borne.'

'How can you defend her when she arranged for the kidnapping of your grandson?' Lisette frowned.

He smiled sadly. 'I am not defending, only understanding.'

Lisette looked at him with the beginning of a grudging affection; Aubrey Maystone might not have been in love with Helene all those years ago, but he had certainly known her— the woman that she had been and still was.

And Lisette…she *could* understand Helene's need, not only for revenge but also for the assistance of the man who had fathered her child twenty years ago.

She understood it, even if she could never have behaved in such a way herself.

'Helene—' Lord Maystone spoke again '—I promise you I would never have abandoned you, or our daughter, if you had once told me of her existence. I will not abandon you now. Either of you,' he added firmly before turning to Christian. 'There will be questions for Helene to answer to the English Crown, but I believe I have enough favours to draw upon to make those questions less…probing than they might otherwise have been. Your brother André was the main conspirator, was he not?' he prompted Helene.

'I tried as best I could to continue his work after he was killed,' Helene stated flatly.

'Did any of your actions succeed?' he mused.

She sighed. 'You know they did not.'

'You arranged for Christian to be shot!' Lisette reminded exasperatedly.

'It was never meant to be a killing shot, Lisette,' Christian said with certainty. 'Am I right, *madame*? You wished only to disable me enough that I must return to England, in the hope I would take Lisette with me?'

Lisette looked round-eyed at her mother. 'Is this true?'

'He is far too intelligent, that one,' Helene muttered.

'That he is.' Maystone nodded with satisfaction. 'I will take it upon myself to explain all to my son and daughter-in-law in regard to the reason Michael was chosen for abduction. After which, I see no reason why Helene should not be allowed to return to Paris. For you to come back to England to visit Lisette occasionally, if that is what you wish. As long as you first make a promise to cease this war against the English Crown,' he added sternly. 'And your personal vendetta against me, of course,' he said with a grimace.

'And Lisette?' Helene prompted huskily.

Lord Aubrey Maystone, the man Lisette now knew to be her father, turned to look at her. 'I believe that must now be for Lisette to decide...'

Lisette looked at the three other people in the room.

Helene, who loved her but was totally incapable of showing that love.

Lord Maystone, who had learned only hours ago that he was her father but already showed a surprising protectiveness towards her, to the extent he had offered himself up to be shot this evening if Helene would only release her.

And Christian.

Christian, of the wicked lavender-coloured eyes.

Christian, of the wicked hands and lips that reduced her to a limp and satiated puddle every time he took her in his arms.

Christian…

A man—the *only* person here—Lisette knew she could trust completely.

The one she could not bear to be parted from.

A fact she had realised during the hours she had been tied and kept prisoner, when she'd had nothing else to entertain her but her own thoughts. A time when she had realised her heart was breaking at the thought she might never look upon Christian's handsome face and those wicked lavender-coloured eyes again.

Because she had fallen in love with him.

Was so much in love with him that she had even offered to become his mistress, if he would have her.

An offer he had refused.

But perhaps if she were to become Lord Maystone's daughter, this English Miss he wished to make of her, then she might still see Christian occasionally?

She did not wish to leave France, but she no

longer had a real home there. Only Helene. But Lord Maystone had said he would arrange it so that Helene and she might see each other sometimes and perhaps, over time, the two of them might come to feel some sort of affection and understanding for each other.

Lisette had no wish to become an English Miss either.

Except...

Except this was where Christian was.

Lisette raised her chin, her decision made.

# Chapter Fifteen

*One month later*

'I hate to say it, old chap, but you have been like a bear with a sore head these past few weeks!' Marcus murmured conversationally as the two men stood at the edge of the dance floor in Maystone's full-to-overflowing ballroom.

Christian's scowl did not lessen in the slightest as he glowered at the young buck twirling past with a glowing Lisette in his arms.

A transformed Lisette, with her fashionably styled red curls and equally fashionable sky-blue silk gown, with matching slippers upon her dainty feet as she danced lightly, and perfectly, by.

She now looked and sounded—he had spoken to her briefly, politely, as she stood at her father's side receiving their guests—every inch the young English society Miss, with not a trace of a French accent to her softly spoken voice, her manner one of perfect politeness.

Tonight was the occasion of Lisette's formal introduction into society, Maystone having decided that, in these unusual circumstances, the 'Little Season' would suit for an introductory ball far better than waiting until next February or March, when the main London Season would begin.

Maystone had organised everything as he had intended, of course. Helene Rousseau had returned to France a few weeks ago, with the blessing of both her daughter and the English Crown. Maystone had resigned his position, and he now spent his time escorting and introducing his young daughter to England and English society.

There had been much talk and speculation these past weeks in regard to the sudden appearance in London of Lord Aubrey Maystone's daughter, and many society families had returned to London for a week or two for the sole purpose of attending this ball, and the opportunity to meet and speak with her.

That the evening was a success could not be doubted, no expense having been spared in Lisette's dress and the beautiful pearls that adorned her ears and her throat, or the champagne and refreshments being served to the guests. Exalted guests, considering there were six Dukes in the room at least; Maystone had invited and made it clear he expected all of the Dangerous Dukes and their wives to attend.

There were also dozens of single young gentlemen literally queuing up to dance with Lisette, or to gather about her when the dancing paused or refreshments were served.

Christian wanted to strangle them all. One by one. Slowly. Thoroughly. Until there was only himself and Lisette left in the room. Perhaps then she might actually say something to him other than, 'Good evening, Your Grace. I am pleased you were able to attend this evening', in that very precise and totally un-Lisette-like English voice.

It had been a little over four weeks—four weeks, three days and two hours, to be precise—since Lisette had made her choice to remain in London and reside at the home of her newly discovered father.

Over four long and tedious weeks—Christian having spent the first frustrating week recovering fully from the wound to his thigh, the following three having been just as frustrating, but in a different way. He had not so much as been able to see or speak a single word alone with Lisette.

Oh, he had called at Maystone House many times once he was fully recovered.

The first time had been in the late morning, and he had been politely shown into the drawing room. Only to then find himself in a room with a genial Maystone and many young and hopeful beaus awaiting the appearance of their young hostess, after having met her the previous evening when she had attended a musical soirée with her father. Lisette had finally arrived, only to ignore his very presence as she sat quietly beside an obviously paternally proud Maystone.

The second time Christian had called it had been in the afternoon, only to learn that Lisette was out at her dressmaker's and not expected back for some time.

The third time had been in the early evening; a time when he had been sure that Lisette must be at home.

He had been wrong.

Miss Maystone, he had been informed by the butler, had gone to the country with her father, to spend the weekend with their family.

That had not been the last of Christian's visits; he had called every two or three days after that, but was always informed that Miss Maystone was either not available or was out.

Leaving Christian to conclude, from the number of times he was fobbed off with one excuse or another, that Miss Maystone had no wish to see him, no matter when he should call.

While Christian was pleased for Lisette that her choice appeared to have been the right one for her, he could not help his own feelings of frustration in not being able to get close enough to so much as speak a private word with her, let alone steal a taste of those delectable pink lips that haunted his dreams every night.

He now turned away from the dance floor and the vision of Lisette laughing gaily up into the handsome face of the young man who was now escorting her back to her father's side.

Lisette was a success.

He should be pleased for her.

He *was* pleased for her.

He was just hellishly miserable for himself. Marcus was right; he had been damned poor company this past month.

But he *missed* Lisette, damn it.

He missed her smile, her impetuosity that had caused her to become involved in so many scrapes—scrapes he had invariably been called upon to rescue her from. He even missed her temper.

Except the Lisette she was now—refined, genteel, every inch the English young lady—no longer appeared to have a temper.

He straightened the cuff of his evening jacket. 'I believe I have had enough for one evening, Marcus. You?'

The other man eyed him impatiently. 'I only came at all because Julianna said that I should, in support of you. We delayed going to the country so that I might attend.' Julianna was now very large with child and would not be out and about in society again until after the babe had been born.

Christian raised haughty brows. 'Support of me?'

Worthing gave an impatient shake of his head. 'You are fooling no one with this act, Christian. If *I* know you are pining for your French *mademoiselle*, then you may be assured that Julianna knew of it long before I did! Besides,' he added slyly, 'Miss Lisette Maystone and my wife are now firm friends.'

*'What?'* Christian could not think of a worse friendship than one between his interfering sister and the irrepressible Lisette. 'How did the two of them even meet?' he demanded irritably.

'My wife deemed it only polite to call upon Miss Maystone and welcome her to London and into society,' Worthing informed him loftily.

Put that way, it was a generous act on Julianna's part; a welcoming visit from the Duchess of Worthing would ensure that all doors in society would be open to Lisette.

Still, Christian could not rid himself of the feeling that a friendship between Julianna and Lisette was a recipe for disaster.

His mouth thinned. 'Whatever you and Julianna are about, Marcus, I advise you to desist. Any attempt to matchmake between myself and Miss Maystone is a complete waste of your own time and mine—'

'No more so than it would be of my own, I do assure you, Your Grace.' An icily haughty voice spoke behind him.

An icily haughty voice that Christian instantly recognised as belonging to Lisette.

Lisette had looked forward to the night of her father's ball with both excitement and trepidation.

Excitement because it was the first ball she had ever attended, and she was to wear a beautiful gown that had been designed and made especially for her for this occasion.

Trepidation because she so longed to see Christian again at the same time as she felt apprehensive about such a meeting.

She had spent the past month becoming the English Miss expected of her as Lord Aubrey Maystone's daughter. Had learned to speak English as clearly and precisely as any in society. Had attended numerous fittings for all the clothes she was assured she would need as a member of that society. Had diligently followed the instructions of her dance instructor, and the teachings of her father in correct manners and conversation.

All of it working towards this single evening.

The evening she was to be with Christian again, when he would see she could be as refined and ladylike as any of the beauties in the society of which he was such a part.

She had worked and struggled hard to become that lady in these four short weeks.

Only to now overhear him dismissing her as if she were no more than a passing acquaintance he had no more regard for than he did all those other silly young debutantes who reputedly threw themselves at him at the start of every Season in the hope of becoming his duchess.

She had felt hopeful as she sensed his gaze upon her throughout the evening, and had deliberately laughed and flirted with all the eligible young gentlemen her father had invited to amuse her. All in the hope that she might pique Christian into inviting her to stand up with him for one dance, at least.

When he had not she had finally decided it was acceptable for her to ask one of the young gentlemen to escort her across the room to speak with Marcus Wilding so that she might enquire about the health of his wife, whom she now counted as her friend. It was no coincidence that Christian stood at that gentleman's side.

The humiliation she now felt, upon hearing Christian's comment to Marcus Wilding, was overwhelming. And made all the more so because Sir Percy Winterbourne, her current escort, had also overheard the derogatory remark.

Christian turned to look at her now, that haughtily superior expression upon his handsome face as he looked down the length of his aristocratic nose at her, those lavender-coloured eyes as cold as ice. 'I merely meant, Miss Maystone, that to add yet another admirer to those already clustered about you would appear to be entirely superfluous,' he drawled mockingly. 'Winterbourne.' He nodded briefly to the man at Lisette's side.

'How true, Your Grace.' Lisette bared her teeth in a smile.

He had bungled this badly, Christian acknowledged with an inward groan of self-disgust. This was the first occasion upon which he had spoken to Lisette away from the watchful eye of her overprotective father, and he had insulted her. Out of self-defence, admittedly, but it was a poor excuse for his rudeness to the young woman who had, he had no doubt, saved his life on more than one occasion, usually to her own detriment.

He drew himself up to his full height. 'I apologise if my remark sounded…less than polite. It was not intended to be, I assure you.'

Lisette looked up at him sceptically. 'Your apology is accepted, Your Grace.'

'Perhaps as confirmation of that acceptance

you might graciously allow me the next dance?'
Christian tensed as he waited for her refusal.

'Oh, but—'

'Been meaning to have a chat with you this evening, Winterbourne—' Marcus Wilding interrupted the younger man's protest '—about that fine piece of horse flesh I saw you on in the park this morning.'

'Really?' The young buck visibly preened at this praise from the Duke of Worthing.

'Oh, yes. Be interested to know where you purchased it.' Worthing continued talking as he first drew the younger man aside before stepping away completely.

'It would seem that Marcus has become as much the matchmaker as my sister.'

Lisette turned to give Christian a scathing glance. 'I assure you, I am no more pleased with this arrangement than you are!'

'Ah, there she is…' Christian murmured with satisfaction.

Her look of scorn turned to a puzzled frown. 'Am I keeping you from someone…?'

'Not at all.' Christian grinned widely; the first

time he could remember doing so for some time. Four weeks, three days and two hours, to be exact.

'I do not understand…'

Christian could not seem to stop himself from grinning. 'I am very pleased, very pleased indeed, to remake your acquaintance, Mademoiselle Duprée.'

'I am Miss Maystone now.' Those blue eyes flashed with impatience. 'And I have been in London these past four weeks, if you had cared to call.'

It was Christian's turn to frown now. 'But I have called upon you. Many times.'

'I do not think so,' Lisette dismissed scathingly. 'I recall only the once, a morning visit in the presence of a dozen other people, when you did not speak so much as a single word to me but stood in a corner of my father's drawing room looking down your haughty nose at everyone!'

'But—' Christian broke off to gaze across to where Aubrey Maystone stood in conversation with the other Dangerous Dukes and their wives. As if aware of his gaze, Maystone glanced across to where Christian and Lisette stood talking together, one iron-grey eyebrow slowly rising in mocking enquiry. 'That wily old fox...' Christian muttered, knowing from the challenging look Maystone was giving him that he was responsible for Lisette not knowing of the many visits Christian had made to Maystone House this past month, his only intention to see her again.

'*Quoi?* I mean, I beg your pardon?' Lisette's cheeks blushed a becoming shade of pink at her mistake in having lapsed into her native French.

Christian gave a roar of laughter, relieved to learn that it had not been Lisette avoiding him after all, but the machinations of her interfering father. His laughter caused more than a few heads to turn in their direction; the Duke of Sutherland was not known for his public displays of levity.

'I fail to see what is so funny in my having let down *mon père* by not speaking the King's English?' Lisette eyed him irritably.

Christian sobered a little. '*Mon père* is not "let down" but is the wily old fox to whom I referred.' He smiled wryly. 'Once a spymaster, always a spymaster, it would seem.'

'Are you quite recovered from your injury, Christian—Your Grace?' Lisette corrected hastily. 'Do you have a fever?' She could think of no other reason for his current strange conversation.

'Would you care to take a stroll out on the terrace with me, Miss Duprée?' He did not wait for her answer before tucking her gloved hand into the crook of his arm and striding off in the direction of the doors opened to prevent the room from becoming too stifling.

'Is such behaviour quite correct, Christian?' Lisette cast a furtive glance at the people she sensed were watching the two of them together, the women from behind their fans, the gentlemen openly speculative of the Duke of Sutherland's obvious intention of stealing their young hostess outside onto the moonlit terrace.

'Correct can go hang, Lisette,' Christian dismissed happily. 'If I do not soon taste your delectable lips and touch your creamy flesh, I am afraid I will do something that will never be forgotten, by not only those members of society present tonight but also the heirs that come after them!'

'Christian!' Lisette gasped her shock.

'Lisette.' He stood aside to allow her to precede him out onto the terrace.

She looked up at him uncertainly, unsure of Christian in this reckless mood. 'My reputation will be ruined if I go outside alone with you.'

'So it will,' he acknowledged unconcernedly.

'Can you possibly have drunk too much champagne this evening?'

'First I am fevered. Then I am accused of neglecting you. Now you believe me to be drunk!' He gave a brief laugh. 'I assure you, my dearest Lisette, I am none of those things,' he added huskily.

'But—'

'My wound is perfectly healed, thanks to your initial diligent care, my doctor has informed me. If I am drunk then it is with the pleasure of being in your company again, for I have not drunk so much as one glass of champagne this evening. As for being neglectful...' He gave a shake of his head. 'I was slightly incapacitated that first week, but I have called at Maystone House every two or three days these past three weeks.'

'I have not seen you…'

'No, you have not,' Christian acknowledged drily. 'And I have not seen you, except at a distance once or twice, as you travelled by in Maystone's coach.' Fleeting glimpses that had reminded him of the last time he and Lisette were in a coach together, those memories leaving him hungering for so much more than a fleeting glimpse of her. 'Please step outside with me, Lisette, and allow me to explain.' He looked down at her intently.

Lisette still eyed him uncertainly, so tempted to do as he asked, at the same time aware of the many eyes upon them as they stood in the open doorway, neither in nor outside of the house. 'What is there to explain?' she prompted slowly.

Christian glanced across at her father, the tension leaving his shoulders as he received a slight nod from the older man. Not that it would have made the slightest difference if he did not have Maystone's blessing, but he was glad of it in any case, for Lisette's sake.

He turned back to her. 'How about what a pompous, blind, ungrateful ass I am?' he began, knowing that Lisette would not have seen the look that passed between the two men.

'Blind and ungrateful how…?'

Christian gave a throaty chuckle. 'I notice you do not question the "pompous" or the "ass"?'

'The first is no doubt because you are a duke. The second…?' She gave one of those achingly familiar Gallic shrugs. 'Perhaps for the same reason?'

Christian choked back another shout of laughter. Indeed he was fast reaching a point where he really would shock all in the room, and to hell with them, their heirs *and* his own. 'Please come outside with me, Lisette,' he pressed urgently.

'If you are merely going to upbraid me for my outspokenness to you just now, or some other social misdemeanour I have made, then I would really rather not—'

'*You* may upbraid me, if you wish,' he asserted fervently. 'For what you have perceived as my tardiness, my neglect and what I now believe to have been my *utter stupidity* in not doing this sooner!'

Lisette gave a gasp as 'this' became Christian sweeping her up into his arms before carrying her outside.

From the ballroom at Maystone House.

For all and everyone in London society to see.

## Chapter Sixteen

'How can you have been so…so *stupide*?' Lisette glared up at Christian in the moonlight bathing the terrace on which they both now stood, the pummelling of her fists upon his chest finally having secured her release. Her cheeks were flushed, her eyes glittering with temper. *'Imbécile!'*

Christian needed no translation of the names Lisette had just called him.

Nor did he say a word to stop her, but simply wallowed in the pleasure of knowing his Lisette was here, after all.

*This* was the Lisette he remembered.

And it was because of her return that he could not regret his actions of a few minutes ago. Damn it, he would have done something very like it long before now, if he had not felt as if Lisette had become a stranger to him.

The musicians had drawn to a discordant halt as they lost their place in the music, to openly stare, along with the rest of the people assembled in Maystone's ballroom, as Christian had swept Lisette up in his arms and carried her out onto the moonlit terrace.

Christian knew the chatter he could now hear above the musicians resuming their playing—no doubt having been encouraged to do so by their host—would all be about the two of them.

Scandalous.

Shocking.

*Damning.*

Very damning for a duke to behave in such a reckless fashion in public.

And Christian did not regret it for a single moment.

How could he, when Lisette was currently berating him, that rapid-fire French he loved to hear spewing forth from those delectable lips.

Instead of being insulted, as she no doubt intended he should be, it was like sweet music to his ears after all these weeks of silence between them.

He leaned back against the balustrade as Lisette paced up and down in front of him, knowing that even she would eventually run out of names to call him.

In the meantime, he could enjoy the sight of her. She really was magnificent when she was in full spate. Her hair seemed a brighter red, eyes sparkling like sapphires, cheeks aflame with colour, her lips a deeper rose, that tiny chin lifted high, her breasts— Ah, those magnificent breasts. *They* were quickly rising and falling above the low neckline of her gown.

Almost indecently so, Christian realised with a frown. Maystone really should not have let Lisette wear a gown with such a scandalously low neckline as this in public. It was the sort of gown that only a lover should see, or a—

'You are not even listening to me. *Imbécile!*'

Ah, Lisette was starting to repeat herself. Time to attempt to redeem himself perhaps—

'No, of course you are not,' she answered her own question impatiently. 'You are the esteemed

Duke of Sutherland; why should it matter to you that you have just completely sullied my reputation—?'

'And my own,' he interjected softly.

'—when men are not held up to the same rules and limitations in English society— *Quoi?*' She frowned as his words finally penetrated her anger.

'I have just sullied my own reputation too, Lisette.' Christian straightened away from the balustrade. 'To such a degree, I believe the only course that might save us both from the derision and pillory of our peers—'

'They are your peers, not mine.' She glared at him. '*I* am not even properly launched into society and already I am ruined. My poor papa must be beside himself!' Her gloved hands twisted together in her agitation.

Christian chuckled softly. 'Unless I am mistaken, your "poor papa" is at this moment filled with self-satisfied jubilation.'

'You really are *ivre*—' She paused, obviously seeking the translation. 'Inebriated. You are inebriated,' she repeated firmly. 'Drunk. Soused—'

'I believe you have made yourself clear, thank you, Lisette,' he drawled. 'And no, I am perfectly sober, I do assure you.'

'Then what on earth possessed you to behave in such a scandalous fashion?'

He shrugged. 'It succeeded in securing your singular attention, did it not?'

Lisette could have cried with pure frustration at the social disaster that had just occurred. All those hours, weeks of excruciating lessons and dress fittings and tedious social visits to her papa's friends, had all been stripped away, demolished by the simple action of Christian sweeping her up in his arms and carrying her from the ballroom.

She would be disgraced, a laughing stock, and her poor papa would never recover from the humiliation caused by his French daughter.

'How could you do such a thing?' Her voice broke emotionally. 'I have tried so hard to be everything that was expected of me. Have suffered through such torments with the dressmakers and milliners and dance instructor, and now it has all been for naught. I am disgraced, will have to retire to the country, become what the English call an Old Maid—' She stopped as Christian gave another roar of laughter.

Indeed, he laughed so loudly and for so long Lisette seriously feared for his sanity.

'Your amusement at my expense is most un-welcome, Christian,' she informed him haughtily when that laughter at last seemed to be abating.

He gave a shake of his head. 'One thing you will never be is an Old Maid, Lisette!'

'You— What are you doing?' she squeaked in surprise as he fell to his knees in front of her. 'You must get up!' She attempted—and failed utterly—to take him by the hands and pull him back up onto his perfectly shod feet. 'I expect only a few words of apology from you, Chris-tian, not this—this— What is it that you are doing?' She frowned her consternation at his unusual behaviour.

'I am trying to ask you to marry me. Not very successfully, I admit,' he acknowledged drily. 'But that could be because the object of my af-fections is too busy berating me to listen to me— Lisette...?' He voiced his concern as she released his hands to stagger away from him until she could go no further, back resting against the balustrade, hand clasped to her breast. 'Lisette—'

'Remain exactly where you are!' She now held her hands up in warning as Christian rose to his feet with the intention of going to her. 'You— This is— I—' She gave a shake of her head. 'You should not play with me in this cruel manner,' she admonished huskily. 'It is wholly unworthy of you.'

Christian tilted his head to one side as he studied the pallor of Lisette's face. Unless he was mistaken, there were tears in those sapphire-blue eyes, her cheeks were pale, her bottom lip trembling slightly, as if she was barely retaining control of those tears.

He stepped forward. 'Maystone should have decked you out in sapphires to match your eyes rather than those pearls.'

'He said—'

'Yes?'

She swallowed. 'He said that it was the role of my future husband to give me sapphires.'

Christian would have fought Maystone for Lisette if he'd had to do so, but he knew in that moment that he had not misunderstood the other man's nod of approval just a short time ago; the Sutherland sapphires—earbobs, a necklace and bracelet—were always given to the new Duchess by her Duke to wear on their wedding day.

'He was quite right; it is.' Christian took another step forward, to stand only inches in front of her. 'I do apologise most sincerely if I embarrassed you with my flamboyant method of leaving the ballroom, Lisette. My only excuse is that I was just so pleased to see you, to be with you again, that I wished to express my joy by holding you in my arms again.'

A frown creased her brow. 'You saw and spoke with me two hours ago when you arrived…'

'I saw and spoke to Miss Lisette Maystone,' he corrected huskily. 'It was *my* Lisette whom I came here to see, and now that I have…' He clasped both her hands in his and fell to his knees in front of her again. 'Lisette—darling, wonderful Lisette—will you marry me and make me the happiest man in England? No, not just England—the whole world!'

It was the second time in as many minutes that Christian had mentioned marriage to Lisette. But he could not seriously be proposing marriage to *her*.

*Could he...?*

Of all the people present here this evening, Christian knew her true story rather than the one that Lord Maystone had chosen to share with society: a tragic tale of love and loss, resulting in him at last being able to claim his long-lost daughter.

Christian *knew* that story to be completely false. Knew too that her mother had been in the past, but was no longer, thank goodness, an enemy to both England and the Crown.

Dukes did not marry women such as she.

Nor, as she knew to her humiliation, did they take them as their mistress either.

She pulled her hands free of his. 'I have no idea why you have chosen to deliberately humiliate and hurt me in this way—perhaps as recompense for my mother's actions last month, I do not know—but I do not deserve such mockery from you. My father certainly does not deserve for you to have behaved in such a fashion in his own home.'

All humour had gone from his expression. 'Your answer is no, then?'

'There was never any real question, so there can be no answer either!' She moved aside and swept past him towards the doorway, and the humiliation that would now be her lot in life.

'Lisette, I love you!'

Lisette froze in the doorway leading back into the ballroom, her breath caught in her throat, her heart pounding loudly in her chest. Seconds later she felt the heat of Christian's body against her back as he moved to stand behind her.

'Lisette, I love you,' he repeated forcefully. 'I want to marry you, to make you my duchess—'

She spun around in his arms, her gloved hands pressed against his chest as she looked up searchingly into his oh-so-handsome and dearly beloved face, the love he proclaimed shining brightly, steadily in his beautiful lavender-coloured eyes.

She swallowed. 'You love me...?'

'I do,' he stated firmly as he took her hands

in his and pressed them to his chest, allowing Lisette to feel the rapid beating of the heart he claimed was hers. 'So much that at this moment I am even prepared to forgive your father for being a wily old fox. Maystone is responsible for us not seeing each other this past month, Lisette,' he explained as she frowned her lack of understanding. 'Every time I called at Maystone House I was either told you were out or unavailable. I believe now that was on your father's instructions.'

She swallowed. 'But why?'

'Because he knew I love you. Marcus knows I love you. Julianna knows I love you. Damn it, I do believe everyone has known I love you except for me!' He gave a self-disgusted shake of his head, his hands tightening about hers. 'Could you not just love me a little bit in return, Lisette?' He looked down at her earnestly. 'I promise if you agree to marry me you will never have cause to regret it. As my duchess you will be the most cherished, the most loved woman in all the world—'

'A duke does not marry a woman like me—'

'What does that even mean?' he dismissed impatiently. 'You are a woman of great courage, honesty and loyalty. A woman who was not afraid to risk her own life to save mine—'

'Helene has said those men were not instructed to kill, only to issue a warning.' Lisette spoke distractedly, huskily, such hope building in her heart she was afraid to let it loose in case her chest was not large enough to contain it.

'*You* did not know that,' Christian insisted. 'Any more than you knew those men would have fled by the time you reached my carriage. You came rushing out into the street anyway, staunched my wound, drove my carriage home, tended my wounds and Pierre's—he is completely recovered, by the way. François sent word just last week.'

'I am glad.' Lisette nodded.

'Lisette…darling Lisette,' Christian groaned. 'I have been such a fool—that arrogant, pompous ass—for not telling you, for not realising how much I love you. I believe I fell in love with you at first sight. I know I could not take my eyes from you, and that I incurred your mother's wrath because of it.' He gave a rueful grimace. 'Each time we met after that I fell a little harder, a little deeper, until my love for you now consumes my every waking moment. I cannot sleep. I cannot eat. Marcus assures me I have been insufferable this past month.'

The hope in Lisette's heart grew to unbearable proportions. 'If you marry me, the illegitimate daughter of Lord Maystone, you will be risking incurring the condemnation of society—'

'I do not give a damn for what society thinks or says.' He waved an impatient hand. 'Besides which, none would dare to gainsay Lord Maystone, his friend the Prince Regent and *all* of the Dangerous Dukes.'

Lisette looked up at him searchingly. 'You believe your friends will publicly support you in this...this endeavour?'

'I know they will,' he asserted without hesitation. 'And it would not matter to me if they did not. I shall marry where and with whom I choose. And I choose you, Lisette. Indeed, if you will not agree to marry me then there will be no Duchess of Sutherland.' His gaze softened.

'Can you not love me just a little in return, Lisette? Will you not marry me and save me from the long and unhappy life of being a Taciturn Bachelor to your Old Maid?'

Hope burgeoned in Lisette's chest, flying free and carrying her with it as she allowed the last of her concerns—for Christian, not for herself—to be satisfied, dismissed as if they had never been.

Christian loved her.

He wished to marry her.

It was more—so very much more—than she had ever dared hope or pray for during this month of not seeing or hearing from him. Her father truly was a 'wily old fox'.

She looked up at him with her own love for him shining brightly in her eyes. 'I believe I have loved you since that first night too, Christian,' she admitted huskily. 'I—'

'You love me?' He pounced eagerly, his hands tightening painfully about hers. 'You *love* me, Lisette?'

'Of course I love you, you silly man.' She reached up to curve her hand lovingly about the hardness of his cheek. 'I love you very much, and of course I will marry you, Christian Algernon Augustus Seaton.'

Christian gave a shout of exultant laughter as he swept her up into his arms and began to kiss her with a thoroughness that took her breath away.

He loved.

And he was loved.

By his outrageous, his darling, his wonderfully unorthodox Lisette.

He asked for no greater happiness than that.

# Epilogue

*Six weeks later, St George's Church, Hanover Square*

'Do stop fidgeting with your necktie, Christian; you are starting to make me feel nervous too!'

Christian gave Worthing a baleful glance as the two of them sat at the front of the church awaiting Lisette's arrival. His beautiful Lisette. Shortly to become his wife, his duchess and his companion for the rest of their lives together.

'I seem to remember you being in just such a state on the day you married my sister Julianna,' he drawled mockingly.

'Yes. Well.' Marcus turned to give his wife an affectionate smile. She sat on the pew just behind them, next to a heavily veiled Helene Rousseau, here today to witness her daughter's wedding.

Julianna had given birth three weeks early to Worthing's son and heir, Peter Matthew Joshua Timothy Wilding. That young man had been left at home with his wet nurse today, but the three would be united following the wedding breakfast.

Christian was amazed at how quickly his brother-in-law had taken to fatherhood, young Peter with his parents constantly when they did not have other commitments.

All of the Dangerous Dukes were present in the church today, along with their wives.

Zachary Black, the Duke of Hawkesmere, and his lovely duchess Georgianna, their baby son also at home with his nanny.

Darian Hunter, the Duke of Wolfingham, along with his beautiful duchess Mariah, their first child due to arrive on Christmas Day.

Rufus Drake, the Duke of Northamptonshire, and his mischievous duchess Anna. Those two had recently learned that their family was also to increase in the spring.

Griffin Stone, the Duke of Rotherham; often too serious in the past, Griffin had at last found true happiness with his duchess Bea. And, from the look of Bea's glow today, Christian would not be at all surprised if the two of them very shortly shared news of their own increasing family.

All of them were here—all of the women having become fast friends, all of the gentlemen having survived their years as agents for the Crown, before just as happily retiring from that endeavour now they had become married men. Some of them were battle-scarred, admittedly, but they had survived and without exception had found their true, their real happiness in the women they loved and who loved them in return.

As Christian had with Lisette.

Which was why he was becoming more and more agitated as the seconds ticked by after the appointed time of twelve o'clock for their wedding ceremony to begin. *Where was she—?*

*Ah.*

Christian breathed a sigh of relief as the organ music began to play in announcement of his bride's arrival, he and Worthing both standing as the Vicar moved into his place at the altar.

It was too much to expect Christian not to turn and look at the woman he loved and who had consented to become his wife, his duchess.

Lisette walked slowly, gracefully on her proudly beaming father's arm, a vision in white, the smile upon her lips only for Christian. The love glowing in her eyes only for him.

His Lisette.

The woman he loved and was about to happily pledge to love and cherish for the rest of their lives together.

* * * * *

# MILLS & BOON®

## Why shop at millsandboon.co.uk?

Each year, thousands of romance readers find their perfect read at millsandboon.co.uk. That's because we're passionate about bringing you the very best romantic fiction. Here are some of the advantages of shopping at www.millsandboon.co.uk:

* **Get new books first**—you'll be able to buy your favourite books one month before they hit the shops

* **Get exclusive discounts**—you'll also be able to buy our specially created monthly collections, with up to 50% off the RRP

* **Find your favourite authors**—latest news, interviews  and new releases for all your favourite authors and series on our website, plus ideas for what to try next

* **Join in**—once you've bought your favourite books, don't forget to register with us to rate, review and join in the discussions

Visit **www.millsandboon.co.uk**
for all this and more today!